# THE ROVER BOYS AT SCHOOL

*By*

## ARTHUR M. WINFIELD

# The Rover Boys at School

## *by* Arthur M. Winfield

Copyright © 2024

ISBN: 978-93-57482-57-8

**Published by**

# DOUBLE 9 BOOKS

2/13-B, Ansari Road, Daryaganj
New Delhi – 110002
info@double9books.com
www.double9books.com
Tel. 011-40042856

# ABOUT THE AUTHOR

Arthur M. Winfield (Edward Stratemeyer) was born on October 4, 1862, to Henry Julius Stratemeyer a tobacconist, and Anna Siegel. He was an American publisher, writer of Children's fiction, and founder of the Stratemeyer Syndicate. He was probably the most creative author in the world, producing over 1,300 books and selling over 500 million copies. He also created many famous fictional book series for juveniles, including The Rover boys, The Bobbsey Twins, Tom Swift, The Hardy boys, and Nancy Drew. As a teenager, Stratemeyer worked at his own printing press in the basement of his father's tobacco shop, distributing flyers and brochures to his relatives. These included stories titled The Newsboys Adventure and The Tale of a Lumberman. After graduating from high school, he worked in his father's shop. He is not even 26 in 1888 while Stratemeyer sold his first story Victor Horton's Idea, to the famous children magazine The Golden Days.

# CONTENTS

# INTRODUCTION

My Dear Boys:

"The Rover Boys at School" has been written that those of you who have never put in a term or more at an American military academy for boys may gain some insight into the workings of such an institution.

While Putnam Hall is not the real name of the particular place of learning I had in mind while penning this tale for your amusement and instruction, there is really such a school, and dear Captain Putnam is a living person, as are also the lively, wide-awake, fun-loving Rover brothers, Dick, Tom, and Sam, and their schoolfellows, Larry, Fred, and Frank. The same can be said, to a certain degree, of the bully Dan Baxter, and his toady, the sneak, commonly known as "Mumps."

The present story is complete in itself, but it is written as the first of a series, to be followed by "The Rover Boys on the Ocean" and "The Rover Boys in the Jungle," in both of which volumes we will again meet many of our former characters.

Trusting that this tale will find as much favor in your hands as have my previous stories, I remain,

Affectionately and sincerely yours,

**EDWARD STRATEMEYER**

# CHAPTER I
## INTRODUCING THE ROVER BOYS

"Hurrah, Sam, it is settled at last that we are to go to boarding school!"

"Are you certain, Tom? Don't let me raise any false hopes."

"Yes, I am certain, for I heard Uncle Randolph tell Aunt Martha that he wouldn't keep us in the house another week. He said he would rather put up with the Central Park menagerie—think of that!" and Tom Rover began to laugh.

"That's rather rough on us, but I don't know but what we deserve it," answered Sam Rover, Tom's younger brother. "We have been giving it pretty strong lately, with playing tricks on Sarah the cook, Jack the hired man, and Uncle Randolph's pet dog Alexander. But then we had to do something—or go into a dry rot. Life in the country is all well enough, but it's mighty slow for me."

"I guess it is slow for anybody brought up in New York, Sam. Why, the first week I spent here I thought the stillness would kill me. I couldn't actually go to sleep because it was so quiet. I wish uncle and aunt would move to the city. They have money enough."

"Aunt Martha likes to be quiet, and uncle is too much wrapped up in the art of scientific farming, as he calls it. I'll wager he'll stay on this farm experimenting and writing works on agriculture until he dies. Well, it's a good enough way to do, I suppose, but it wouldn't suit me. I want to see something of life—as father did."

"So do I. Perhaps we'll see something when we get to boarding school."

"Where are we to go?"

"I don't know. Some strict institution, you can be sure of that. Uncle Randolph told aunty it was time the three of us were taken in hand. He said Dick wasn't so bad, but you and I—"

"Were the bother of his life, eh?"

"Something about like that. He doesn't see any fun in tricks. He expects us to just walk around the farm, or study, and, above all things, keep quiet, so that his scientific investigations are not disturbed. Why doesn't he let us go out riding, or boating on the river, or down to the village to play baseball with the rest of the fellows? A real live American boy can't be still all the time, and he ought to know it," and, with a decided shake of his curly head, Tom Rover took a baseball from his pocket and began to throw it up against the side of the farmhouse, catching it each time as it came down.

Tom had thrown the ball up just four times when a pair of blinds to an upper window flew open with a crash, and the head of a stern-looking elderly gentleman appeared. The gentleman had gray hair, very much tumbled, and wore big spectacles.

"Hi! hi! boys, what does this mean?" came in a high-pitched voice. "What are you hammering on the house for, when I am just in the midst of a deep problem concerning the rotation of crops on a hillside with northern exposure?"

"Excuse me, Uncle Randolph, I didn't think to disturb you," answered Tom meekly. "I'll put the ball away."

"You never stop to think, Thomas. Give me that ball."

"Oh, let me keep it, Uncle Randolph! I won't throw it against the house again, honor bright."

"You'll forget that promise in ten minutes, Thomas; I know you well. Throw the ball up," and Mr. Randolph Rover held out his hands.

"All right, then; here you go," answered Tom, somewhat put out to thus lose a ball which had cost him his week's spending, money; and he sent the sphere flying upward at a smart speed. Mr. Rover made a clutch for it, but the ball slipped through his hands and landed plump on his nose.

"Oh!" he cried, and disappeared from sight, but reappeared a moment later, to shake his fist at Tom.

"You young rascal! You did that on purpose!" he spluttered, and brought forth his handkerchief, for his nose had begun to bleed. "Was anyone ever tormented so by three boys?"

"Now you are in for it again, Tom," whispered Sam.

"I didn't mean to hit you, Uncle Randolph. Why didn't you catch it on the fly?"

"On the fly?" repeated the uncle. "Do you suppose I am accustomed to catching cannon balls?"

"Didn't you ever play baseball?"

"Never. I spent my time in some useful study." The elderly gentleman continued to keep his handkerchief to his nose, and adjusted his glasses.

"Thank fortune, you are all going to go to boarding school next week, and we will once more have a little peace and quietness around Valley Brook!"

"Where are we to go, Uncle Randolph?" asked Sam.

"You will learn that Monday morning, when you start off."

"It wouldn't hurt to tell us now," grumbled Tom.

"You must learn to be patient, Thomas. My one hope is that life at boarding school makes a real man of you."

"Of course we are all to go together?"

"Yes, you are to go together, although I can get along with Richard very well, he is so much more quiet and studious than you or Samuel."

"I reckon he takes after you, Uncle Randolph."

"If so, he might do worse. By the way, what were both of you doing here?"

"Nothing," came from Sam.

"We haven't anything to do. This farm is the slowest place on earth," added Tom.

"Why do you not study the scientific and agricultural works that I mentioned to you? See what I have done for scientific farming."

"I don't want to be a farmer," said Tom. "I'd rather be a sailor."

"A sailor!" gasped Randolph Rover. "Of all things! Why, a sailor is the merest nobody on earth!"

"I guess you mean on the sea, uncle," said Sam with a grin.

"Don't joke me, Samuel. Yes, Thomas—the calling of a sailor amounts to absolutely nothing. Scientific farming is the thing! Nothing more noble on the face of the earth than to till the soil."

"I never saw you behind a plow, Uncle Randolph," answered Tom, with a twinkle in his blue eyes. "Besides, I heard you say that the farm ran behind last year."

"Tut, tut, boy! You know nothing about it. I made a slight miscalculation in crops, that was all. But this year we shall do better."

"You lost money year before last, too," commented Sam.

"Who told you that?"

"Mr. Woddie, the storekeeper at the Corners."

"Mr. Woddie may understand storekeeping, but he knows nothing of farming, scientific or otherwise. I spent several thousands of dollars in experimenting, but the money was not lost. We shall soon have grand results. I shall astonish the whole of New York State at the next meeting of our agricultural society," and Mr. Randolph Rover waved his hand grandiloquently. It was easy to see that scientific farming was his hobby.

"Randolph!" It was the voice of Mrs. Rover, who now appeared beside her husband. "What is the matter with your nose?"

"Tom hit me with his ball. It is all right now, although it did bleed some."

"The bad boy! But it is just like him. Sarah has given notice that she will leave at the end of her month. She says she can't stand the pranks Tom and Sam play on her."

"She need not go—for the boys are going to boarding school, you know."

"She says you promised to send them off before."

"Well, they shall go this time, rest assured of that. I cannot stand their racing up and down stairs, and their noise, any longer. They go Monday morning."

"Better send them off tomorrow."

"Well—er—that is rather sudden."

"Sarah's month is up Friday. She will surely go unless the boys are out of the house. And she is the best cook I have ever had."

"Excepting when she burnt the custard pies," put in Tom.

"And when she salted the rice pudding!" added Sam.

"Silence, both of you. Randolph, do send them off."

"Very well, I will. Boys, you must go away from the house for an hour or two."

"Can we go fishing or swimming?" asked Tom.

"No, I don't want you to go near the river, you may get drowned."

"We can both swim," ventured Sam.

"Never mind—it is not safe—and your poor father left you in my care."

"Can we go down to the village?"

"No, you might get into bad company there."

"Then where shall we go?" came from both boys simultaneously.

Randolph Rover scratched his head in perplexity. He had never had any children of his own, and to manage his brother's offspring was clearly beyond him. "You might go down to the cornfield, and study the formation of the ears—"

"Send them blackberrying," suggested Mrs. Rover. "We want the berries for pies tomorrow, and it will give them something to do."

"Very well; boys, you may go blackberrying. And mind you keep out of mischief."

"We'll mind," answered Tom. "But you might let me have that ball."

"I will give it to you in the morning," answered Randolph Rover, and turned away from the window with his wife.

As soon as they were out of sight, Tom threw up both hands in mock tragedy, "Alack, Horatio, this excitement killeth me!" he cried in a stage whisper. "Sent blackberrying to keep us out of mischief! Sam, what are we coming to?"

"Well, it's better than moping around doing nothing. For my part, I am glad we are to go to boarding school, and the sooner the better. But I would like to know where to?"

"If only we were going to a military academy!"

"Hurrah! Just the thing! But no such luck. Get the berry baskets and let us be off. By the way, where is Dick?"

"Gone to the village for the mail. There he comes down the road now," and Tom pointed to a distant path back of the meadows.

The two boys hurried into a woodshed behind the large farmhouse and procured a basket and two tin pails. With these in hand they set off in the direction of the berry patch, situated along the path that Dick Rover was pursuing, their intention being to head off their brother and see if he had any letters for them.

Of the three Rover boys, Richard, commonly called Dick, was the eldest. He was sixteen, tall, slender, and had dark eyes and dark hair. He was a rather quiet boy, one who loved to read and study, although he was not above having a good time now and then, when he felt like "breaking loose," as Tom expressed it.

Next to Richard came Tom, a year younger, as merry a lad as there was ever to be found, full of life and "go," not above playing all sorts of tricks on people, but with a heart of gold, as even his uncle and aunt felt bound to admit.

Sam was the youngest. He was but fourteen, but of the same height and general appearance as Tom, and the pair might readily have been taken for twins. He was not as full of pranks as Tom, but excelled his brothers in many outdoor sports.

The history of the three Rover boys was a curious one. They were the only children of one Anderson Rover, a gentleman who had been widely known as a mineral expert, gold mine proprietor, and traveler. Mr. Anderson Rover had gone to California a poor young man and had there made a fortune in the mines. Returning to the East, he had married and settled down in New York City, and there, the three boys had been born.

An epidemic of fever had taken off Mrs. Rover when Richard was but ten years of age. The shock had come so suddenly that Anderson Rover was dazed, and for several weeks the man knew not what to do. "Take all of the money I made in the West, but give me back my wife!" he said broken-heartedly, but this could not be, and soon after he left his three boys in charge of a housekeeper and set off to tour Europe, thinking that a change of scene would prove a benefit.

When he came back he seemed a changed man. He was restless, and could not remain at home for more than a few weeks at a time. He placed the boys at a boarding school in New York and returned to the West, where he made another strike in the gold mines; and when he came back once more he was reported to be worth between two and three hundred thousand dollars.

But now a new idea had came into his head. He had been reading up on Africa, and had reached the conclusion that there must be gold in the great unexplored regions of that country. He determined to go to Africa, fit out an exploration, and try his luck.

"It will not cost me over ten to twenty thousand dollars," he said to his brother Randolph. "And it may make me a millionaire."

"If you are bound to go, I will not stop you," had been Randolph Rover's reply. "But what of your boys in the meanwhile?"

This was a serious question, for Anderson Rover knew well the risk he was running, knew well that many a white man had gone into the interior of Africa never to return. At last it was settled that Randolph Rover should become Dick, Tom, and Sam's temporary guardian. This accomplished, Anderson Rover set off and that was the last any of his family had ever heard of him.

Was he dead or alive? Hundreds of times had the boys and their uncle pondered that question. Each mail was watched with anxiety, but day after day brought no news, until the waiting became an old story, and all settled down to the dismal conviction that the daring explorer must be dead. He had landed and gone into the interior with three white men and twenty natives, and that was all that could be ascertained concerning him.

At the time of Anderson Rover's departure Randolph had been on the point of purchasing a farm of two hundred acres in the Mohawk Valley of New York State. The land had not changed hands until a year later, however, and then Dick, Tom, and Sam were called upon to give up their life in the metropolis and settle down in the country, a mile away from the village of Dexter Corners.

For a month things had gone very well, for all was new, and it seemed like a "picnic," to use Tom's way of expressing it. They had run over the farm from end to end, climbed to the roof of the barn, explored the brook, and Sam had broken his arm by falling from the top of a cherry tree. But after that the novelty wore away, and the boys began to fret.

"They want something to do," thought Randolph Rover, and set them to work studying scientific farming, as he called it. At this Dick made some progress, but the uncle could do nothing with Tom and Sam. Then the last two broke loose and began to play pranks on everybody that came along, and life became little short of a burden to the studious Randolph and, his quiet-minded spouse.

"I must send them off to a boarding school, or somewhere," Randolph Rover would say, but he kept putting the matter off, hoping against hope that he might soon hear from his lost brother.

# CHAPTER II
## AN ENCOUNTER ON THE ROAD

"I'll race you to the path," said Sam, when the woodshed was left behind.

"All right," answered Tom, who was always ready to run. "Toe the mark here. Now then—one, two, three! Go!"

And away they went across the meadow, leaping two ditches with the agility of a pair of deer, and tearing through the small brush beyond regardless of the briers and the rents their nether garments might sustain. At first Tom took the lead, but Sam speedily overhauled and then passed him.

"It's no use—you always could outrun me," panted Tom, as he came to a stop when Sam crossed the footpath ten yards ahead of him. "I can't understand it either. My legs are just as long as yours, and my lungs just as big, too, I think."

"You want to do your running scientifically, Tom. That athletic instructor in New York—"

"Oh, bother your scientific things, Sam! Uncle gives us enough of that, so don't you start in. I wonder if Dick has got a letter from Larry Colby? He promised to write last week. He is going to a boarding school soon."

"We'll know in a few minutes. I wonder where Larry—Gracious, listen!"

Sam broke off short, as a loud cry for help reached their ears. It came from the footpath, at a point where it ran through a grove of beech trees.

"It's Dick's voice! He wants help!" burst from Tom's lips. "Come on!" and he set off as rapidly as his exhausted condition would permit. As before, Sam readily outdistanced him, and soon came upon the scene of a most brutal encounter.

A burly tramp, all of six feet in height, had attacked Dick Rover and thrown him upon his back. The tramp was now kneeling upon the prostrate boy's chest, at the same time trying to wrench a watch from Dick's vest pocket.

"Keep still there, or I'll knock you on the head!" cried the tramp, as, letting go of the watch chain, he clapped a dirty hand over Dick's mouth.

"I—won't—kee—keep still!" spluttered Dick. "Let—me—up!"

"You will keep still—if you know what is best for you. I have your pocketbook, and now I am bound to have that watch and that ring."

"No! Don't rob me of the watch! It belonged to my father!" panted Dick, and as the watch came out of the pocket he made a clutch at it. "Help! help!"

"Will you shut up!" burst out the tramp fiercely, and struck at the youth with his fist.

It was at this juncture that Sam put in an appearance. A glance told him how matters stood, and without waiting an instant he came up behind the tramp, and, catching him by the shoulders, hurled him backward.

"Sam! Good for you!" burst out Dick joyfully. "Don't let him get away!"

"What do you mean, boy?" demanded the ruffian, as he turned over and leaped to his feet.

"You let my brother alone—that's what I mean," was the answer.

"Give me my pocketbook and that watch!" went on Dick, for the tramp held both articles, one in each hand.

"Yes, I will—not," was the ready reply, turning, suddenly, the tramp started through the grove of trees on a run.

Without waiting, Sam ran after him followed by Tom, who had now arrived. Dick came behind, too much winded by being thrown on his back to keep up with them.

"He is making for the river!" cried Tom, after running for several minutes without gaining on the thief. "If he has a boat he'll get away!

"I don't think he has a boat, Tom. He looks like a regular tramp."

"We'll soon find out."

They could not see the ruffian, but they could hear him quite plainly as he crashed through the brush beyond the grove of trees. Then came a crash and a yell of pain.

"He has stumbled and fallen!" said Sam, and redoubled his speed. Soon he reached the spot where the tramp had gone down. He was about to proceed further when a well-known object caught his eye.

"Here is the pocketbook!" he burst out, and picked the article up. A hasty examination showed that the contents were intact; and the two boys continued the pursuit, with Dick still following.

They were now going downhill toward the river, and presently struck a patch of wet meadow.

"We must be careful here," observed Tom, and just then sank up to his ankles in water and mud. But the tramp could now be seen heading directly for the river, and they continued to follow him.

They were still fifty yards from the shore when Sam uttered a cry of dismay. "He's got a boat!"

"So he has. Stop there, you thief!"

"Stop yourself, or I'll shoot one of you!" growled the tramp, as he leaped into a flat bottom craft moored beside a fallen tree. He had no pistol, but thought he might scare the boys.

They came to a halt, and an instant later the flat-bottom craft shot away from the river bank. By this time Dick came up, all out of breath.

"So he has gotten away!" he cried in dismay.

"Yes," answered Sam, "but here is your pocketbook."

"And what of my watch—the one father gave to me before he left for Africa?"

"He's got that yet, I suppose," said Tom.

At this Dick gave a groan, for the watch was a fine gold one which Mr. Rover had worn for years. Dick had begged for the timepiece, and it had been entrusted to him at the last moment.

"We must get that watch back somehow!" he said. "Isn't there another boat around here?"

"There is one up to Harrison's farm."

"That is quarter of a mile away."

"I don't think there is any nearer."

"And the river is all of two hundred feet wide here! What shall we do?"

It was a puzzling question, and all three of the boys stared blankly at each other. In the meantime, the thief had picked up a pair of oars and was using them in a clumsy fashion which showed plainly that he was not used to handling them.

"If we had a boat we could catch him easily," observed Tom. Then his eyes fell upon the fallen tree. "I have an idea! Let us try to get across on that! I won't mind a wetting if only we can get Dick's watch back."

"Yes, yes; just the thing!" put in his elder brother quickly.

All hands ran down to the fallen tree, which was about a foot in diameter and not over twenty-five or thirty feet in length. It lay half in the water already, and it was an easy matter to shove it off.

"We can't do much without oars or a pole," said Tom. "Wait a moment," and he ran back to where he had seen another fallen tree, a tall, slender maple sapling. He soon had this in hand; and, cleared of its branches, it made a capital pole. Dick and Sam sat astride of the tree in the water, and Tom stood against an upright branch and shoved off. The river was not deep, and he kept on reaching bottom without difficulty.

By this time the tramp was halfway across the stream, which was flowing, rapidly and carrying both boat and tree down toward a bend quarter of a mile below.

"Go on back, unless you want to be shot!" cried the man savagely, but they paid no attention to the threat as no pistol appeared; and, seeing this, the thief redoubled his efforts to get away.

He was still a quarter of the distance from the opposite shore, and the boys on the tree were in midstream, when Sam uttered a shout. "There goes one of his oars! We can catch him now—if we try hard!"

It was true that the oar was gone, and in his anxiety to regain the blade the tramp nearly lost the second oar. But his efforts were unavailing, and he started to paddle himself to the bank, meanwhile watching his pursuers anxiously.

"We'll get him," said Dick encouragingly, when, splash! Tom went overboard like a flash, the lower end of his pole having slipped on a smooth rock of the river bottom. There was a grand splutter, and it was fully a minute before Tom reappeared—twenty feet away and minus his pole.

"Hi! help me on board, somebody!" he spluttered, for he had gone overboard so quickly that he had swallowed a large quantity of water.

Both Sam and Dick tried to reach him, but could not. Then the current caught the tree and whirled it around and around until both boys began to grow dizzy.

Seeing they could not aid him, and getting back a little of his wind, Tom struck out for the tree. But the water running over his face blinded him, and ere he knew he was so close the tree came circling around and struck him on the side of the head.

"Oh!" he moaned, and sank from sight.

"Tom's hit!" gasped Sam. "He'll be drowned sure now!"

"Not if I can help him!" burst out Dick, and leaped overboard to his brother's assistance. But Tom was still out of sight, and for several seconds could not be located.

Sam waited anxiously, half of a mind to jump into the river himself. The tramp was now forgotten, and landed on the opposite bank unnoticed. He immediately dove into the bushes, and disappeared from view.

At last Dick caught sight of Tom's arm and made a clutch for it. Hardly had he taken hold than Tom swung around and caught him by the throat in a deathlike grip, for he was too bewildered to know what he was doing.

"Save me!" he groaned. "Oh, my head! Save me!"

"I will, Tom; only don't hold me so tight," answered Dick. "I—can't get any air."

"I can't swim—I'm all upset," was the reply; and Tom clutched his elder brother tighter than ever.

Seeing there was no help for it, Dick caught hold of the fingers around his throat and forced them loose by main force. Then he swung himself behind Tom and caught him under the arms, in the meantime treading water to keep both of them afloat.

"Sam, can't you bring that tree closer?" he called out.

There was no reply, and, looking around, he saw that the tree and his younger brother were a hundred yards away, and sailing down the river as rapidly as the increasing current could, carry them for quarter of a mile below were what were known as the Humpback Falls—a series of dangerous rapids through which but few boats had ever passed without serious mishap.

"I reckon Sam is having his hands full," he thought. "I must get Tom to the shore alone. But it is going to be a tough job, I can see that."

"Oh, Dick!" came from Tom. "My head is spinning like a top!"

"The tree hit you, Tom. But do keep quiet, and I'll take care of you."

"I can't swim—I feel like a wet rag through and through."

"Never mind about swimming. Only don't catch me by the throat again, and we'll be all right," was Dick's reassuring reply, and as his brother became more passive he struck out for the bank upon which the thief had landed.

The current carried them on and on, but not so swiftly as it was carrying the tree. Soon they were approaching the bend. Dick was swimming manfully, but was now all but exhausted.

"You can't make it, Dick," groaned Tom. "Better save yourself."

"And let you go? No indeed, Tom. I have a little strength left and—Hurrah, I've struck bottom!"

Dick was right: his feet had landed on a sandbar; and, standing up, both boys found the water only to their armpits. Under such circumstances they waded ashore with care, and here threw themselves down to rest.

"That thief is gone," said Dick dismally.

"And my watch too!"

"But where is Sam?" questioned Tom, then looked at his brother meaningfully.

"The Humpback Fall!" came from Dick. "Sam! Sam!" he yelled; "look out where you are going!"

But no answer came back to his cry, for Sam had long since floated out of hearing.

# CHAPTER III
## SAMS ADVENTURE AT HUMPBACK FALLS

For several minutes after Dick leaped overboard to Tom's assistance, Sam's one thought was of his two brothers. Would they reach the tree or the shore in safety? Fervently he prayed they would.

The tree went around and around, as a side current caught it, and presently the whirlings became so rapid that Sam grew dizzy, and had to hold tight to keep from falling off.

He saw Dick catch Tom from the back and start for shore, and then like a flash the realization of his own situation dawned upon him. He was on the tree with no means of guiding his improvised craft, and sweeping nearer and nearer to the rapids of which he had heard so much but really knew so little.

"I must get this tree to the river bank," he, said to himself, and looked around for some limb which might be cut off and used for a pole.

But no such limb was handy, and even had there been there would have been no time in which to prepare it for use, for the rapids were now in plain sight, the water boiling and foaming as it darted over one rock and another, in a descent of thirty feet in forty yards.

"This won't do!" muttered the boy, and wondered if it would not be best to leap overboard and try to swim to safety. But one look at that swirling current made him draw back.

"I reckon I had best stick to the tree and trust to luck to pass the rocks in safety," he muttered, and clutched the tree with a firmer hold than ever.

The strange craft had now stopped circling, and was shooting straight ahead for a rock that stood several feet above water. On it went, and Sam closed his eyes in expectancy of an awful shock which would pitch him headlong, he knew not to where.

But then came a swerve to the left, and the tree grated along the edge of the rock. Before Sam could recover his breath, down it went over the first line of rapids. Here it stuck fast for a moment, then turned over and went on, throwing Sam on the under side.

The boy's feet struck bottom, and he bobbed up like a cork. Again he clutched the tree, and on the two went a distance of ten feet further. But now the tree became jammed between two other rocks, and there it stuck, with Sam clutching one end and the water rushing in, a torrent over the other.

For the moment the boy could do little but hold fast, but as his breath came back to him he climbed on top of the tree and took a look at the situation.

It was truly a dismaying one. He was in the very center of the rapids, and the shore on either side of him was fifty to sixty feet away.

"How am I ever to get to the bank?" he asked himself. "I can't wade or swim, for the current is far too strong. I'm in a pickle, and no mistake. I wonder if Dick and Tom are on solid earth yet?"

He raised his voice into a shout, not once, but several times. At first only the echoes answered him, but presently came a reply from a distance.

"Sam! Sam! Where are you?" It was Dick calling, and he was running along the bank alone, Tom being too exhausted to accompany him.

"Here I am—in the middle of the falls!"

"Where?"

"Out here—in the middle of the falls!"

"Great Caesar, Sam! Can't you wade ashore?"

"No; the current is so strong I am afraid to."

In a minute more Dick reached a spot opposite to where the tree rested. As he took in the situation his face clouded in perplexity.

"You are right—don't try wading," he, said. "If you do, you'll have your skull cracked open on the rocks. I'll have to get a rope and haul you off."

"All right; but do hurry, for this tree may start on again at any instant!"

To procure a rope was no easy matter, for nothing of that sort was at hand, and the nearest farmhouse was some distance away. Yet, without thinking twice, Dick set off for the farmhouse, arriving there inside of five minutes.

"I need a rope, quick, Mr. Darrel," he said. "My brother is in the middle of the Humpback Falls on a tree, and I want to save him."

"Why, Dick Rover, you don't tell me!" cried Joel Darrel, a farmer who had often worked for Randolph Rover. "Sure I'll get a wash line this minute!" and he ran for the kitchen shed.

Luckily the line was just where the farmer supposed it would be, and away went man and boy, Dick leading, until the river bank was again reached.

"There he is, Mr. Darrel. How can we best help him, do you think?"

The farmer scratched his head in perplexity.

"Hang me if I jess know, Dick," he said slowly.

"If we try to pull him straight to shore the current will carry him over the rocks in spite of the line."

"How long do you suppose the line is?"

"It is fifty yards, and all good and strong, for I bought it of Woddie only last week."

"Fifty yards—that is a hundred and fifty feet. Do you see that spur of rock just above there?"

"I do."

"Is it more than a hundred and fifty feet from that rock to the tree?"

"Hardly; but it's close figuring."

"Let us try the line and see."

Both walked up to the spur of rock they had in view. It jutted out into the river for several yards, and was rather wet and slippery.

"Take care, or you'll go in too," cautioned Joel Darrel. "Shall I throw the rope out?"

"You might try it," answered Dick. "I'll hold fast to your leg," and he squatted down for that purpose.

The line was uncoiled and thrown three times, but each time it fell short and drifted inshore again.

"Hurry up!" suddenly yelled Sam. "The tree is beginning to turn, and it will break loose before long."

"Let me try a throw," said Dick, and took the wash line. As he made the cast, Tom came up on a walk, his head tied up in a handkerchief.

"Where is Sam?"

"Out there," said Joel Darrel, and watched the casting of the line with interest. Again it fell short, but Dick's second throw was a complete success, and soon Sam held the outer end of the line fast.

"It reaches, and we have about fifteen feet to spare," said Dick joyfully. "Sam, tie it around you." Scarcely had the word left the younger brother's lips than the tree upon which he rested wobbled and went over, and he found himself thrown into the foaming water.

"Pull away, all hands!" cried Dick, and hauled in desperately, while Joel Darrel did the same. Tom was not equal to the task, but contented himself with holding fast to Dick's coat, that his elder brother might not slip from the rock.

It was no light work to get Sam up the first rise of the rapids, but once this rise was passed the rest was easy by comparison. They pulled in steadily, and presently the boy reached the rock and came up, looking very much like a dripping seal as he clambered to safety.

"Thank fortune, you are safe!" cried Dick when it was all over; and Tom said "Amen," under his breath. Joel Darrel looked well satisfied as he coiled up the wash line.

"It was a narrow escape," he remarked presently. "You want to be careful how you try to cross the river at this point. What were you doing on the tree?"

"I was after a thief," answered Sam, and then he looked at Dick and Tom. "Where is he?"

"Gone," returned Dick.

"A thief!" ejaculated Joel Darrel. "Whom did he rob?"

"He robbed me."

"Do tell, Dick! When?"

"About half an hour ago. I was coming from the Corners with the mail, when he pounced on me near our berry patch and knocked me down. He took my pocketbook and my watch, but Sam and Tom came up, and we chased the fellow and got the pocketbook back."

"But he kept the watch?"

"Yes."

"Was it a good one?"

"It was a gold watch that my father paid sixty-five dollars for—and the chain was worth ten; and, what is more, the watch was one my father used to wear; and as he is gone now, I thought a good deal of it on that account."

"That's natural, my boy. But where did the thief go?"

"Came across the river about quarter of a mile above here."

"Then he had a boat?"

"Yes—a craft painted brown, with a white stripe around her."

"That's Jerry Rodman's boat. He must have stolen her in the first place to cross to your side."

"More than likely."

"But where did he go after he crossed the river?"

"Into the bushes, I guess. You see, Tom went overboard from the tree and got struck, and I went to his assistance, so I didn't notice exactly. I want to get back now and follow the rascal."

"I'll go along."

"I wish you would."

"In that case I won't try to keep up with you," put in Tom. "My head is aching fit to split."

"Yes, you may as well take it easy," answered Dick. "But, say, why not, walk up to the river road and see if the rascal heads in this direction?"

"So I will, Dick. Will you go too, Sam?"

It was arranged that Sam should accompany and they set off immediately, while Dick and Joel Darrel ran along the river bank to where the rowboat had been abandoned.

Down where it was muddy it was easy to trace the tramp's footprints, and they led through a meadow and across a cornfield, coming out at a side road leading to the town of Oak Run.

"Well, where to next?" questioned the farmer, as he and Dick came to a halt.

The youth shook his head. "It's so dry here the footprints are lost," he returned slowly.

"That's true, Dick. But I reckon he went to Oak Run."

"Why?"

"Because he could catch a train from there which would take him miles away—and I guess that is what he wants to do just about now."

"There is something in that."

"Besides, you know, the other end of the road ends up in the woods. He wouldn't go there."

"I had best start for Oak Run, then."

"I'll go along."

The distance was a mile and a half, and they thought they would have to walk it, but hardly had a dozen rods been covered than they heard the sound of wagon wheels, and a grocery turnout and came into sight driven by a boy Joel Darrel knew well.

"This comes in just right," observed Darrel to Dick. "Hi there, Harry Oswald. Give us a lift to Oak Run, will you?"

"Certainly, Mr. Darrel," answered the grocery boy, and brought his store wagon to a stop. The farmer leaped to the seat, and Dick followed.

On the way Harry Oswald was made acquainted with the situation, and he drove along with all possible speed. They were just entering the outskirts of Oak Run when the whistle of a locomotive was heard.

"That's the down train for Middletown," cried Joel Darrel. "Hurry up!"

The horse was whipped up, and they swept along to the depot at a speed which made the constable of the town shake his fist at Harry and threaten to arrest him for fast driving.

"Too late!"

The words came from Dick, and he was right. Before the depot was reached the long train had pulled out. Soon it was lost to sight in the distance.

The thief was on it; and his escape, for the time being, was now assured.

# CHAPTER IV
# THE LAST DAY AT THE FARM

"What does this mean?"

It was Gilbert Ponsberry, the chief constable of Oak Run, who spoke, as he strode up to the grocery wagon, all out of breath.

"Hullo, Ponsberry, you are just the man we want to see!" cried Joel Darrel. "Did you notice who boarded that train?"

"No; I wasn't at the depot. Anything wrong?"

"I have been robbed of a gold watch and chain," answered Dick, and related the particulars.

"Gee shoo! No wonder you drove fast," ejaculated the constable. "I would have done so myself. How did that fellow look?"

As well as he was able, Dick gave a description of the thief.

"I saw that tramp yesterday," said the constable, when he had finished. "He was in the depot, talking to a tall, thin man. I remember him well, for he and the other fellow were quarreling. I hung around rather expecting a fight. But it didn't come."

"You haven't seen the thief since yesterday?"

"No."

"You remember the tall, thin man he was with?"

"Oh, sure, for he had a scar on his chin that looked like a knife cut."

"Is he anywhere around?"

"I haven't seen him since. Let us take a walk around, and we can ask Ricks the station master about this."

"We had better ask Mr. Ricks first," said Dick.

All hands, even to the grocery boy, hunted up the station master, an elderly fellow who was well known for his unsociable disposition.

"Don't know anything about any thief," he snapped, after hearing the story. "I mind my own business."

"But he may have taken the train," pleaded Dick. It made his heart sink to think that the watch, that precious memento from his father, might be gone forever.

"Well, if he did, you had better go after him—or telegraph to Middletown," was the short answer, and then the station master turned away.

"You telegraph for me," said Dick to the constable. "I will pay the costs."

"All right, Dick. My, but old Ricks is getting more grumpy every day! If this railroad knows its business it will soon get another manager here," was Gilbert Ponsberry's comment, as he led the way to the telegraph office.

Here a telegram was prepared, addressed to the police officer on duty at the Middletown station, and giving a fair description of the thief.

The train would reach the city in exactly forty-five minutes; and as soon as the message had been sent, Dick, Darrel, and the constable went off on a tour of Oak Run and the vicinity.

Of course nothing was seen of the thief, and in an hour word came back from Middletown that he was not on the cars.

This was true, for the train had stopped at a way station, having broken something on the engine, and the thief had left, to walk the remainder of the distance to Middletown on foot.

It was not until nightfall that Dick returned to his uncle's farmhouse.

Here he found that Sam and Tom had already arrived. Tom was lying on the sofa in the sitting room, being cared for by his Aunt Martha, who was the best of nurses whenever occasion required.

"Didn't find any trace of the villain?" queried Randolph Rover, with a sad shake of his head. "Too bad! Too bad! And it was your father's watch, too!"

"I never wanted to see Dick wear it," put in Mrs. Rover. "It was too fine for a boy."

"Father told me to wear it, aunty. He said it would remind me of him," answered Dick, and he turned away, for something like a tear had welled up in his eye.

"There, there, Dick, I didn't mean to hurt your feelings," cried his aunt hastily. "I would give a good deal if you had your watch back."

Supper was waiting, but Dick had no appetite, and ate but little. Tom braced up sufficiently to take some toast and tea, and declared that he would be all right by morning and so he was.

"Here is a letter for Tom from Larry Colby," cried Dick during the course, of the evening.

"I declare, I forgot all about it, Tom, until this minute."

"I don't blame you, Dick," was the reply, with a sickly smile. "You read it for me. The light hurts my head," and Tom closed his eyes to listen.

Larry Colby was a New York lad who in years gone by had been one of Tom's chums. The letter was just such a one as any boy might write to another, and need have no place here. Yet one paragraph interested everybody in the sitting room:

"Next week I am to pack my trunk and go to Putnam Hall Military Academy [wrote Larry Colby]. Father says it is a very fine military, school, and he has recommended it to your uncle."

"Putnam Hall Military Academy!" mused Tom. "I wonder where it is?"

"It is over in Seneca County, on Cayuga Lake," replied Randolph Rover, and something like a smile appeared on his face.

"On Cayuga Lake, uncle!" cried Sam. "Why, that's a splendid location, isn't it?"

"Very fine."

"And is that where we are to go?" put in Tom eagerly.

"Yes, Thomas; I might as well tell you, although I wanted to surprise you. You are to go to Putnam Hall, and there you will have with you Lawrence Colby, Frank Harrington, and several other lads with whom you are all acquainted."

"Hurrah, Uncle Randolph!" came from Sam, and rushing up, he caught his relative around the shoulder. "You're the best kind of uncle, after all."

"Putnam Hall is an institution of learning that has been established for some twenty years," went on Mr. Rover, pushing back his spectacles and laying down the agricultural work he had been perusing. "It is presided over by Captain Victor Putnam, an old army officer, who in his younger days used to be a schoolmaster. He is a strict disciplinarian, and will make you toe the mark; but let me say right here, I have it from Mr. Colby that there is no schoolmaster who is kinder or more considerate of his pupils."

"Is it a regular military institution like West Point?" asked Tom.

"Hardly, Thomas, although the students, so I am informed, dress like cadets and spend an hour or so each day in drilling, and in the summer all the school march up the lake and go into an encampment."

"That just suits me!" broke in Sam enthusiastically. "Hurrah for Putnam Hall!"

"Hurrah!" echoed Tom faintly, and Dick nodded to show he felt as they did. At the cheer, Sarah the cook stuck her head into the door.

"Sure an' I thought Tom was out of his head, bedad," she observed.

"Sarah, I'm going away soon—to a military academy. I won't bother you any more," said Tom.

"Won't yez now? That will be foine." Then the cook stopped short, thinking she had hurt the boy's feelings. "Oh, Master Tom, don't moind me. You're not such an—an awful bother as we think," and then at a wave of Mrs. Rover's hand she disappeared.

After this the evening passed quickly enough, for the boys wanted to know all there was to be learned about their future boarding school. Mr. Rover had a circular of the institution, and they pored over this.

"Captain Victor Putnam is the head master," said Dick, as he read. "He has two assistants, Josiah Crabtree and George Strong, besides two teachers who come in to give instructions in French and German if desired, also in music. Uncle Randolph, are we to take up these branches?"

"I am going to leave you to select your own studies outside of the regular course, Richard. What would be the use of taking up music, for instance, if you were not musically inclined."

"I'd like to play a banjo," said Tom, and grinned as well as the bandage on his head, would permit.

"I doubt if the professor of music teaches that plantation instrument," smiled Mrs. Rover. Then she patted Tom's shoulder affectionately.

Now the boys were really to leave her, she was sorry to think of their going.

"They will not take more than a hundred pupils," said Dick, referring to the circular again. "I should say that was enough. The pupils are divided into two companies, A and B, of about fifty soldiers each; and the soldiers elect their own officers, to serve during the school term. Tom, perhaps you may turn out captain of Company B."

"And you may be Major Dick Rover of the first battalion," returned Tom. "Say, but this suits me to death, Uncle Randolph."

"I am glad to hear it, Thomas. But I want you to promise me to attend to your studies. Military matters are all well enough in their way, but I want you to have the benefits of a good education."

"Oh, I fancy Captain Victor Putnam will attend to that," put in Sam.

The circular was read from end to end, and it was after ten o'clock before the boys got done talking about it and went to bed. Certainly the prospect was a bright one, and if poor Dick had only had his watch the three would have been in high feather. Little did they dream, of all the startling adventures in store for them during their term at Putnam Hall.

It must not be supposed that Mr. Randolph Rover intended to allow the theft of Dick's watch to pass without a strong effort being made to recover the article. Early in the morning he drove to the Corners, and to Oak Run and another village called Bender's, and at each place had a notice posted, mentioning the loss and offering a reward of fifty dollars for the recovery of the property and of one hundred dollars if the thief was captured in addition. This offer, however, proved of no avail, and Dick had to leave for Putnam Hall wearing his old silver watch, which he had put aside upon the receipt of the gold timepiece.

It was a clear, sun-shiny morning when the boys started off. They had paid a last visit to the various points of interest about the place and bid good-by to Sarah, who shook hands warmly, and said farewell to the hired men, both of whom hated them to leave, for they had made matters pleasant as well as lively. Their three trunks were loaded in a farm wagon, and now Jack, one of the men-of-all-work, drove up with the two seated carriage to drive them over to Oak Run by way of the river bridge, half a mile up the stream.

"Good-by, Uncle Randolph!" cried one after another, as they shook hands. "Good-by, Aunt Martha!" and each gave Mrs. Rover a hug and a kiss, something which brought the tears to the lady's eyes.

"Good-by, boys, and take good care of yourselves," said Randolph Rover.

"And if you can't stand it at boarding school, write, and we will send for you to come back here," added his wife; and then, with a crack of the whip, the carriage rolled off, and the farm was left behind. It was to be many a day before the boys would see the place again.

# CHAPTER V
## ON THE WAY TO PUTNAM HALL

"I don't think we'll want to send word to Aunt Martha to be taken back," observed Sam, who sat on the driver's seat with the hired man.

"Neither do I," returned Tom. "To be sure, we have a nice enough home here, but it's dreadfully slow."

"There is no telling what may be in store for us," joined in Dick. "Don't you remember how Fred Garrison fared at Holly School? That institution sent out a splendid circular, and when Fred got there they almost starved him to death."

"That is true. Where is Fred now?"

"I don't know."

"Mr. Colby wouldn't recommend Putnam Hall if it wasn't all right," remarked Tom. "Jack, whip up the team, or we'll miss that train."

"They are going putty well now, Master Tom," replied the driver.

The trunks had gone on ahead, and when they reached the depot at Oak Run they found old Ricks grumbling because no one was there to check them.

"Do you reckon I'm going to be responsible for everybody's baggage?" he snarled as Dick approached him.

"I'll check them as soon as I can get tickets," answered Dick curtly. "What an old bear he is!" he whispered to Tom. "He didn't treat me half decently when I was over here about the watch."

"If only we had a little time I would fix him," whispered Tom in return. He had sobered down for several days now and was dying to play a trick on somebody.

They went into the station and procured tickets, and then found the time for the train had been changed, and it would not be along for nearly half an hour.

"Good! Just wait till I get back," said Tom.

He had noticed Ricks gathering up some waste paper around the depot, and felt tolerably certain the old fellow was about to build a bonfire of it. Walking over to one of the stores, he entered, and asked the proprietor if he had any large firecrackers on hand.

"Just two, sir," said the storekeeper, and brought them forth. Each was six inches long and thick in proportion.

"How much?" asked the boy.

"Seeing as they are the last I have, I'll let you have them for fifteen cents each."

"I'll give you a quarter for the two."

"Very well; here you are," and the transfer was made on the spot. Slipping the firecrackers into his coat pocket, Tom sauntered up to old Ricks, while Sam and Dick looked on, sure that something was in the wind.

"Ricks, that is pretty bad news from Middletown, isn't it?" he observed.

"Bad news? What do you mean?" demanded the station master, as he threw some more waste paper on the fire, which he had just lit.

"About that dynamite being stolen by train wreckers. They think some of the explosive was brought up here."

"Didn't hear of it."

"Dynamite is pretty bad stuff to have around, so I've heard."

"Awful! Awful! I never want to see any of it," answered Ricks, with a decided shake of his head.

"If it goes off it's apt to blow everything to splinters," went on Dick.

"That's so—I don't want any of it," and the old man began to gather up more waste paper for his fire. Watching his chance, Tom threw one of the firecrackers into the blaze and then rejoined his brothers.

With a handful of paper Ricks again approached the blaze. He was standing almost over it when the firecracker went off, making a tremendous report and scattering the light blazing paper in all directions.

"Help! I'm killed!" yelled old Ricks, as he fell upon his back. "Get me away from here! There's dynamite in this fire!" And he rolled over, leapt to his feet, and ran off like a madman.

"Don't be alarmed—it was only a firecracker," called out Tom, loud enough for all standing around to hear, and then he ran for the train, which had just come in. Soon he and his brothers were on board and off, leaving poor Ricks to be heartily laughed at by those who had observed his sudden terror. It was many a day before the cranky station master heard the last of his dynamite.

The boys were to ride from Oak Run to Ithaca, and there take a small steamer which ran from that city to the head of the lake, stopping at Cedarville, the nearest village to Putnam Hall. At Cedarville one of the Hall conveyances was to meet them, to transfer both them and their baggage to the institution.

The run to Ithaca proved uneventful although the boys did not tire of looking out of the window at the beautiful panorama rushing past them. At noon they had lunch in the dining car, a spread that Sam declared was about as good as a regular dinner. Three o'clock in the afternoon found them at the steamboat landing, waiting for the Golden Star to take them up to Cedarville.

"Fred Garrison, by all that's lucky!" burst out Tom suddenly, as he rushed up to a youth of about his own age who sat on a trunk eating an apple.

"Tom Rover! Where are you bound?"

"To a boarding school called Putnam Hall."

"You don't say! Why, I am going there myself," and now Fred Garrison nearly wrung off Tom's hand.

"If this isn't the most glorious news yet!" burst in Dick. "Why, Larry Colby is going too!"

"I know it. But he won't come until tomorrow."

"And Frank Harrington is going too."

"He is there, already—he wrote about it day before yesterday. That makes six of us New York, boys."

"The metropolitan sextet," chirped in Sam.

"Boys, we ought to form a league to stand by each other through thick or thin."

"I'm with you on that," answered Fred. "As we are all newcomers, it's likely the old scholars will want to haze us, or, something like that."

"Just let them try it on!" cried Tom. "Yes, we must stick together by all means." And the compact, so far as it concerned the Rover boys and Fred Garrison, was made on the spot. Later on Larry Colby and Frank Harrington joined them gladly.

It was not long before the Golden Star, a stanch little side-wheeler, steamed up to the dock, and the waiting crowd rushed on board and secured favorable places on deck. The baggage followed, and soon they were off, with a whistle which awoke the echoes of Cayuga Lake for miles around.

While waiting on the dock Dick had noticed three girls standing near them. They were evidently from the rural district, but pretty and well dressed. The boys took seats near the bow of the boat, on the upper deck, and presently the girls sat down not far away.

"He was awfully bold, Clara; I want nothing to do with him," Dick heard the prettiest of the girls say. "He had no right to speak to us."

"He had dropped his handkerchief, and he pretended I was stepping on it," said another of the three. "Oh, here he comes now!" she went on as a youth of seventeen came into view. He was large and bold-looking, and it was easy to see that there was a good deal of the bully about him. He was smoking a cigarette, but on seeing the girls he threw the paper roll away.

"How do you do again?" he said, as he came up and tipped his hat.

At this all of the girls looked angry, and not one returned his salutation. But, undaunted by this, the newcomer caught up a camp stool and planked himself down almost directly between the prettiest of the three and her companions.

"Splendid day for the trip," he went on.

"Won't you have some confectionery?" and he hauled from his pocket a box of cream chocolates and held them out.

"Thank you, but we don't wish any," said the youngest of the girls.

"Won't you have some?" asked the unknown of the eldest girl.

"I don't want any, and I told you before not to speak to me!" she said in a low voice, and the tears almost came into her eyes.

"I ain't going to hurt you," grumbled the young fellow. "Can't a fellow be pleasant like?"

"I do not know you, sir."

"Oh, that's all right. My name is Daniel Baxter. Sorry I haven't a card, or I would give you one," was the smooth rejoinder.

"I do not wish your card," was the answer delivered in the most positive of tones.

"Oh, all right. Yes, it's a splendid trip," said the fellow, and drew his camp chair even closer. The girls wished to edge away, but there was no room in the narrow bow. The eldest girl looked around as if for help. Her eyes met those of Dick, and she blushed.

"Say, that fellow is a regular pill," whispered Tom to his elder brother.

"Somebody ought to take him by the collar and pitch him overboard."

"You are right, Tom," answered Dick, and then as the bully attempted to crowd still closer to the girls he suddenly arose, took a few steps forward, and caught Dan Baxter by the arm.

"You get out of here and be quick about it," he said in low but firm tones.

The fellow started, and for the instant his face changed color. But then he saw that Dick was but a boy, younger and smaller than himself, and his bullying manner returned. "Who are you talking to?" he demanded.

"I am talking to you. I told you to get out—and be quick about it."

"Oh," cried the eldest girl, but her face took on a look of relief, for she saw that Dick was a thoroughly gentlemanly youth.

"Who are you anyway?" blustered Dan Baxter.

"My name is Dick Rover, if you want, to know." Dick turned to the girls. "He was annoying you, wasn't he?"

"Very much," answered the three promptly.

"Then you'll get out, Daniel Baxter."

"Supposing I refuse?"

"If you refuse, I'll pitch you out, and make a complaint to the police at our first stopping place."

"You talk big!" sneered the bully, but he was much disconcerted.

"Don't you talk back to my brother," put in Tom, who had come up. "You think you're a regular masher, as they call such silly fellows, but I don't think your game is going to work here."

"That's it," chimed in Sam.

"Humph! three of you, eh?" muttered the bully. "We'll see about this some other time," and leaving his camp chair he made for the cabin and disappeared, from view.

"He's a bad egg," was Tom's comment, but how thoroughly bad the Rover boys were still to learn.

# CHAPTER VI
## FRIENDS AND ENEMIES

"I must thank you for ridding us of that fellow," said one of the girls. "He has annoyed us several times."

"It was a pleasure to assist you," answered Dick, with the politeness of a dancing master, and tipped his hat; and his brothers and Fred Garrison did the same.

After this there seemed nothing to do but to be introduced, and Dick did this for the boys, while the eldest girl acted for herself and her companions.

"My name is Dora Stanhope," she said. "These are my cousins Nellie and Grace Laning. We live at Cedarville."

"Just the place we are going to!" cried Tom. "We are bound for Putnam Hall. I suppose you know the place?"

"We do—very well," answered Dora Stanhope. "It is less than quarter of a mile away from our farm."

"And it is quite near to our place too," added Nellie Laning.

"Then perhaps we'll see more of each other," remarked Fred Garrison.

"Perhaps; but isn't Captain Putnam rather strict about letting you boys out?" questioned, Dora.

"We don't know yet—we are newcomers."

"Newcomers!" cried Nellie. "Then you don't know that fellow who was just here?"

"No. Does he belong at Putnam Hall?"

"Yes. I know nothing of him, however, further than that I have seen him several times on the Hall road."

Dick gave a low whistle.

"Perhaps we've put our foot in it," remarked Sam in a low tone to him.

"Never mind; we did what was right," answered Dick. "No fellow is justified in acting as Dan Baxter did."

"That's right."

"Tell us something about Putnam Hall, won't you?" said Fred Garrison, after a pause.

At this the three girls laughed.

"What should we know about that place?" asked Dora. "We have never been inside, excepting at one Christmas entertainment."

"But you must see some of the fellows occasionally."

"Not often," said Grace Laning. "Captain Putnam does not allow his pupils to leave the grounds excepting on special occasions. But papa caught three of the pupils in our strawberry patch once."

"He did? And what happened to the fellows?" put in Tom with deep interest.

"Father made them pick twelve quarts of berries for him for nothing, and didn't let them eat a single one."

"Great Caesar! What a fine fellow your dad—I mean your father—must be."

"Of course he is fine. The boys had no right to attempt stealing the berries. My father would have given them some for the asking."

"But they wouldn't have been half as sweet as if they were hooked on the sly," said Tom wisely, and everybody laughed.

"You boys ought to have fine times at Putnam Hall," went on Dora to Dick. "I sometimes see the soldier boys marching; and once, last summer, I visited their encampment."

"We are looking forward to a good time,'" was the answer. "And I trust we see you again," went on Dick; and Dora blushed prettily.

The Golden Star was now approaching a little landing known as Hopedale, and all left their chairs to see the village, and people getting on and off. It was an engaging scene, and the did not return to the bow of the boat until ten minutes later, after taking a walk completely around the steamer's deck.

In the bow a surprise awaited them. During their absence Dan Baxter had appropriated four of their camp chairs and was stretched out on them as if in sleep.

"Oh, what a cheek!" cried Tom.

"Let us haul him off," suggested Sam.

"All right, come ahead," put in Fred.

"Oh, please don't have another row with him!" cried Dora in alarm. "Let him keep the seats. We can go somewhere else."

"All right, let the pig sleep," said Dick.

He felt tolerably certain that Dan Baxter was awake and heard him, but the bully made no sign.

The party walked away, and the bully sneered softly to himself.

"They didn't dare to tackle me," was what he thought in his conceit. "I'd like to meet 'em one by one alone. I'd show each a trick or two."

At last Cedarville was reached and the little steamer tied up at the dock, and the boys and girls went ashore. Just before leaving, Dick took a look at Dan Baxter and saw that he was now sleeping in earnest.

"I won't wake him," he thought. "If he is carried to the head of the lake, it will only serve him right."

Once on the dock, he and Fred hurried off to see about the baggage, and while they were gone a well-dressed and pleasant-looking farmer came up and kissed each of the girls. It was Mr. Laning.

"I hope you had a nice visit to Cousin May's," he said. "Come, the carriage is waiting out in the street."

And he hurried the girls away before they had hardly time to say good-by.

"Nice girls," remarked Tom.

"Yes, indeed," answered Sam. "Hope we see them again."

"We won't have much of a chance if what they say about Putnam Hall is true, Sam. Evidently Captain Putnam believes in keeping his pupils well in hand."

"Well, Uncle Randolph believes we ought to be taken well in hand."

Dick and Fred returned presently, bringing with them a tall, lean man of apparently fifty.

"Boys," cried Fred, "let me introduce you to Mr. Peleg Snugsomebody, general utility man at Putnam Hall."

"Peleg Snuggers, please," said the man meekly. "Excuse me, but I was sent to bring you to the Hall."

"Do we walk?" demanded Tom.

"No, sir; the carryall is out on the street, and my boy Pete has the wagon for your trunks."

"The trunks are already in the wagon," said Dick. "Come ahead."

"How many of you, please?" went on Peleg Snuggers.

"There is only one of me, thank you," answered Tom meekly.

"Don't joke me so early in the term, please," said the utility man pleadingly. "Goodness knows, I'll get more than my share between now and Christmas. I mean, how many it the party?"

"Five of us, Mr. Sluggrub."

"Snuggers, please; Peleg Snuggers—an easy name to remember when you get the swing of it, sir."

"To be sure, Smullers. Yes, there are exactly five of us," and Tom winked at his companions.

"That's all right; the captain said to bring five. Where is the other?"

"What other?"

"The other boy. I see only four of you."

"You asked me how many there were in the party, Mr. Snugbug."

"Yes, sir; and you said five."

"Four of us, and only one of you. Isn't that five—or do they have a different kind of arithmetic at Putnam Hall from what I have been studying?"

"Please don't joke, Master Rover, please don't. I was to bring five boys." The utility man drew a slip of paper from his pocket. "Four new boys—Richard, Samuel, and Thomas Rover and—Frederick Garrison—and Corporal Daniel Baxter."

"Gracious, the bully is a corporal at the Hall!" came from Sam in so low a tone that Snuggers did not catch it.

"The corporal isn't present," said Fred, gazing around absently.

"So he isn't. Must have missed the boat. Come along, please," and Peleg Snuggers led the way to where a large and extra-heavy carryall stood. A splendid team of iron-grays was attached to the carriage; and Dick, who loved good horseflesh, could not help but admire the animals.

"Oh, they are fine, Master Richard," said Snuggers. "Nothing finer on the lake shore. Captain Putnam's one recreation is to drive behind a fast team."

"Is it? I wish he would take me out with him some time."

"Always drives alone. Reckon it kind of quiets him, after a noisy time with the boy."

"I suppose."

They were soon on the way, which led out of Cedarville and over a hill fronting the lake.

"By the way, do you know where the farms belonging to Mr. Stanhope and to Mr. Laning are located?" asked Tom, when they were well out of the village.

"Mr. Stanhope, sir? There isn't any Mr. Stanhope. He died two years ago. That place you see away over yonder is Mrs. Stanhope's farm."

"She has a daughter Dora?"

"Yes," Peleg Snuggers paused for a moment. "They say the widder thinks of marrying again."

"Is that so!" put in Dick, and then he wondered if Dora would be pleased with her stepfather. "So that is the place?"

"Yes, sir; two hundred and fifty acres, and the fittest dairy in these parts. If the widder marries again, her husband will fall into a very good thing. The dairy company at Ithaca once offered fifty thousand dollars for the cattle and land."

"Gracious!" came from Tom. "We've been chumming with an heiress. Are the Lanings rich, too?"

"Very well to do. That is their place, that side road. Here is where we turn off to get to the Hall. Captain Putnam had this road made when the Hall was first built."

The road was one of cracked stone, as smooth as a huge iron roller could make it. They bowled along at a rapid rate, under the wide spreading branches of two rows of stately maples. They were close to the lake, and occasional glimpses of water could be caught through the tree branches.

"It is certainly a splendid locality for a boarding academy," was Dick's comment. "My, what pure air—enough to make a sick boy strong! Do you have much sickness at the Hall?"

"Very little, sir. The captain does not let a cast of sickness stand, but calls in Dr. Fremley at once."

"That is where he is level-headed," said Fred. "My father said I was to call for a doctor the minute I felt at all sick."

They were now approaching Putnam Hall, but there was still another turn to make. As they swept around this, they came upon a tramp, half asleep under a tree. The tramp roused up at the sounds of carriage wheels and looked first at the driver of the carryall and then at the four boys.

"Phew!" he ejaculated, and lost no time in diving out of sight into some brush back of the row of maples.

"Hullo, who was that?" cried Sam.

"A tramp, I reckon," answered the utility man. "We are bothered a good deal with them."

"Begging at the Hall for the left-overs?"

"Exactly. The captain is too kind-hearted. He ought to drive 'em all away," answered Peleg Snuggers; and then the carryall passed on.

When it was gone, and the wagon with the trunks had followed, the tramp came out of the brush and gazed after both turnouts. "Say, Buddy Girk, but dat was a narrow escape," he muttered to himself. "Wot brought dem young gents to dis neighborhood? It can't be possible da have tracked me—an' so quick." He hesitated. "I t'ink I had better give dis neighborhood de go-by," and he dove into the brush again. He was the rascal who had stolen Dick's timepiece.

# CHAPTER VII
## TOM GETS INTO TROUBLE

Putnam Hall was a fine building of brick and stone, standing in the center of a beautiful parade ground of nearly ten acres. In front of the parade ground was the wagon road, and beyond was a gentle slope leading down to the lake. To the left of the building was a playground hedged in by cedars, at one corner of which stood a two-story frame building used as a gymnasium. To the right was a woods, while in the rear were a storehouse, a stable, and several other outbuildings, backed up by some farm lands, cultivated for the sole benefit of the institution, so that the pupils were served in season with the freshest of fruits and vegetables.

The Hall was built in the form of the letter F, the upright line forming the front of the building and the other lines representing wings in the rear. There were three entrances—one for the teachers and senior class in the center, one for the middle classes on the right, and another for the youngest pupils on the left. There were, of course, several doors in the rear in addition.

The entire ground floor of the Hall was given over to class and drill rooms. The second floor was occupied by Captain Putnam and his staff of assistants and the pupils as living and sleeping apartments, while the top floor was used by the servants, although there were also several dormitories there, used by young boys, who came under the care of Mrs. Green, the housekeeper.

Captain Victor Putnam was a bachelor. A West Point graduate, he had seen gallant service in the West, where he had aided the daring General Custer during many an Indian uprising. A fall from a horse, during a campaign in the Black Hills, had laid him on a long bed of sickness, and had later on caused him to retire from the army and go back to his old profession of school teaching. He might have had a position at West Point as an instructor, but he had preferred to run his own military academy.

"Hurrah, here we are at last!" cried Fred Garrison, as the carryall swept into view of the Hall. "I see twenty or thirty of the students, and all togged out in soldier clothes!"

"I suppose we'll be wearing suits soon,", answered Tom. "By George! I'm going to give them a salute."

(For the doings of the Putnam Hall students previous to the arrival at that institution of the Rover boys see "The Putnam Hall Series," the first volume of which is entitled, "The Putnam Hall Cadets."—Publishers)

"How?" asked Sam.

"Never mind. Just wait and see."

In a minute more they swept up to the gateway leading to the parade ground. Some of the pupils had seen the carriage coming, and they ran down to learn if any old friends had arrived.

"Hullo!" yelled several.

"Hullo yourself!" came in return, and then Tom drew out the firecracker still in his pocket and lit it on the sly. Just as it was about to explode he threw it up into the air.

Bang! The report was loud and clear, and everybody within hearing rushed to the spot to see what it meant. There were forty or fifty pupils and two assistant teachers, but Captain Putnam had gone out.

"Hi! Hi! What does this mean?" came in a high-pitched voice, and Josiah Crabtree, the first assistant, rushed up to the carryall. "What was that exploded?"

"A big firecracker, sir," answered Peleg Snuggers.

"And who exploded it?"

Before the utility man could answer there came a cry from the parade ground:
"Don't peach, Peleg, don't peach!"

"Silence, boys!" burst from Josiah Crabtree wrathfully. "Such a disturbance is against the rules of this institution."

"We didn't fire the cracker," piped up a tall, slim boy. "It came from the carriage."

"Mumps, you're nothing but a sneak and tattle-tale," was the reply to this, from several older cadets; and, afraid of having his ears boxed on the sly, John Fenwick, nicknamed Mumps by everybody in the Hall, ran off.

"Which of you fired the cracker?" demanded Josiah Crabtree, advancing to the carriage step.

There was no reply, and he turned to the driver.

"Snuggers, what have you to say?"

"I can't say anything, sir. I was taking care of the horses, sir," answered the hired man meekly.

"I will find out who fired the cracker before I have finished with you," growled the head assistant. "Get down and march into the Hall."

"Gracious, what have we struck now?" whispered Fred to Dick.

"Is this Captain Putnam?" asked Dick, without answering his chum.

"No, young man; I am Josiah Crabtree, A. M., Captain Putnam's first assistant. And you are—" He paused.

"I am Dick Rover, sir. These are my brothers, Tom and Sam."

"And I am Fred Garrison," finished that youth.

"Very good. I hope, Richard, that you were not guilty of firing that cracker?"

"Was there any great harm in giving a... a salute upon our arrival?"

"Such a thing is against the rules of the institution. Article 29 says, 'No pupil shall use any firearms or explosive at any time excepting upon special permission'."

"We are not pupils yet, Mr. Crabtree."

"That argument will not pass, sir. So you fired the cracker?
Very well. Mr. Strong!"

The second assistant came up. He was a man of not over twenty-five, and his face was mild and pleasant.

"What is it, Mr. Crabtree."

"You will take charge of the other new pupils, while I take charge of the one who has broken our rules on his very arrival."

"Hold on!" cried Tom. "What are you going to do with my brother?"

"That is... none of your business, Master Rover. You will go with Mr. Strong."

"He didn't fire the cracker. I did that! And I'm not ashamed of it. I wasn't a pupil when I did it, and I'm not a pupil now, so I can't see how you can punish me for breaking one of your rules."

At this there came a titter from the cadets gathered around. Hardly any of them liked Josiah Crabtree, who was dictatorial beyond all reason. The head assistant flushed up.

"You are a pupil here, and I will show you that you cannot break our rules with impunity, and be impudent to me in the bargain!" cried Crabtree. "Come with me!" And he caught Tom by the arm, while Dick and the others were led off in another direction.

"Surely, this is a fine beginning," thought Tom as he walked along. He was half inclined to break away, but concluded to await developments.

"Are you going to take me to Captain Putnam?" he questioned.

"We do not permit cadets placed under arrest to ask questions."

"Great smoke! Am I under arrest?"

"You are."

"Perhaps you'll want to hang me next."

"Silence! Or I shall be tempted to sentence you to a caning."

"You'll never cane me, sir."

"Silence! You have evidently been a wayward boy at home. If so it will be best for you to remember that all that is now at an end, and you must behave yourself and obey orders."

"Can't a fellow breathe without permission?"

"Silence!"

"How about if I want a drink of water?"

"Silence, I say!" stormed Josiah Crabtree. "I'll warrant you'll not feel so smart by the time you are ready to leave Putnam Hall."

There was a silence after this, as the head assistant led the way into the building and conducted Tom to a small room looking out toward the rear.

"You will remain here, Rover, until Captain Putnam returns."

"How long will that be?"

"Didn't I tell you not to ask questions?"

"But Captain Putnam may not return for a day or a month," went on Tom innocently.

"Captain Putnam will be back in an hour or two." Without another word, Josiah Crabtree turned and left the room, locking the door behind him.

"Well, by crickety!" came from the boy when he was left alone. "I've put my foot into it from the very start. I wonder what Captain Putnam will say to this? If he's half as sour minded as old Crabtree, I'll catch it. But I haven't done anything wrong, and they shan't cane me—and that's flat!" and he shook his curly head decidedly.

The room was less than ten feet square and plainly furnished with two chairs and a small couch. In one corner was a washstand containing a basin and a pitcher of water.

"This looks a good deal like a cell," he mused as he gazed around. Suddenly his eyes caught some writing on the wall in lead pencil. He stepped over to read it.

"Josiah Crabtree put me here,
And I am feeling very queer;
He boxed my ears and pulled my hair
Oh, when I'm free won't I get square!"

"Somebody else has been here before me," thought Tom. "I rather reckon I'll get square too. Hullo, here's another Whittier or Longfellow:

"In this lock-up I'm confined;
If I stay long I'll lose my mind.
Two days and nights I've paced the floor,
As many others have before."

"I hope I don't stay two days and nights," said Tom half aloud. Then he walked to the single window of the apartment to find that it was heavily barred.

"No escaping that way," he went on to read another inscription, this time in blank verse:

"And I am jugged,
Alone in solitude, and by myself
Alone. I sit and think, and think,
And think again. Old Crabtree,
Base villain that he is, hath put me here!
And why? Ah, thereby hangs a tale, Horatio!
His teeth, the teeth that chew the best of steak
Set on our table—those I found and hid;
And Mumps, the sneak, hath told on me! Alas!
When will my martyrdom end?"

"Good for the chap who hid the teeth!" continued Tom, and smiled as he thought of the rage Crabtree must have been in when he discovered that his false teeth were gone. A rattle in the keyhole disturbed him, and he dropped onto a chair just as the head assistant again appeared.

"I want the keys to your trunk and your satchel," he said.

"What for, sir?"

"Didn't I tell you before not to ask questions?"

"But my keys are my own private property, and so is what is in the trunk and the satchel."

"All pupils' baggage is examined, Rover, to see that nothing improper is introduced into the Hall."

"Want to see if I've got any more firecrackers?"

"We do not allow dime novels, or, eatables, or other things that might harm our pupils."

"Eating never harmed me, sir."

"Sometimes parents load up their boys with delicacies which are decidedly harmful. Come, the keys."

Josiah Crabtree's tones were so harsh that Tom's heart rebelled on the moment.

"I shan't give them to you, Mr. Crabtree. You have no right to place me here. I wish to see the proprietor, Captain Putnam, at once."

"Do you—er—refuse to recognize my authority over you?" cried Josiah Crabtree passionately.

"I do, sir. When I have met Captain Putnam and been enrolled as a cadet it may be different. But at present I am not a cadet and not under your authority."

"We'll see, boy, we'll see!" came hotly from the head assistant. "Before I am done with you, you will be sorry that you have defied me!"

And with these words he went out, slamming the door after him. Tom had made an enemy at the very start of his career as a cadet.

# CHAPTER VIII
## A MEETING IN THE MESSROOM

In the meantime Dick, Sam, and Fred had been having quite a different experience. George Strong, the second assistant at Putnam: Hall, was not only a first-class teacher, but a calm and fair-minded gentleman as well; and in addition, and this was highly important, he was not so old but that he could remember perfectly well when he had been a boy himself.

"Come this way, my lads," he said with a faint smile. "I trust you will soon feel at home in Putnam Hall. It is Captain Putnam's desire to have all of his boys, as he calls them, feel that way."

"What will Mr. Crabtree do with my brother?" asked Dick anxiously.

"I cannot say, Rover. Probably he will place him in the guardroom until Captain Putnam arrives."

"I am sure he didn't do much that was wrong."

"We had better not discuss that question, my boy. Come this way; I will conduct you to your room."

"George Strong showed them into the main hallway and up the stairs to the second story. Passing through a side hall, they entered a large, bright dormitory overlooking the parade- and the playground. Here were eight beds, four on either side, with as many chairs, and also a table and two washbowls, with running water supplied from a tower on the roof, the water being pumped up by the aid of a windmill.

"This room has not been occupied this year," said the teacher. "Captain Putnam and Mrs. Green, our housekeeper, thought it might be as well to put you in here together, along with Lawrence Colby and Frank Harrington, when they come. I believe you are all friends, at least Harrington and Colby intimated as much in their letters."

"They told the truth," cried Sam. "This just suits me, and we owe Captain Putnam and Mrs. Green one for doing it."

George Strong smiled. Then the smile faded as he remembered how Josiah Crabtree once told Captain Putnam that he did not believe in letting chums room together. "Place each boy among strangers," Crabtree had said. "It will make him more reliant." But Captain Putnam had not listened to the crabbed old fellow, and Strong was glad of it.

"Here is a closet, in which each of you can stow his clothing when it is dealt out to him. Your ordinary suits will, of course, be placed away for you, for during the academy term, you will as cadets wear only your uniforms."

"When will I get my uniform?" asked Fred, who was anxious to don his "soldier fixings," as he put it.

"Tomorrow, if we have any suit on hand that fits."

"I don't want a second-handed suit," put in Sam.

George Strong laughed. "Don't worry, my boy; every pupil gets new clothing. But, many boys are so nearly of a size that Captain Putnam always keeps a dozen or more suits on hand."

"Oh, that's different."

"The beds are all numbered, and to avoid disputes we always put the eldest boy in bed No. 1, and so on. You can arrange this between yourselves, and I feel certain you won't get into a dispute."

"We won't quarrel," said Dick. "I don't how exactly how old Frank and Larry are, though."

"Then arrange to suit yourselves until they come," concluded Mr. Strong.

Having shown then their dormitory he conducted them through the building and exhibited the various class- and drill-rooms, and then ended up by introducing them to several other pupils, including Bart Conners, the major for the term, and Harry Blossom and Dave Kearney, the two captains.

"Welcome to Putnam Hall!" cried Major Bart Conners, a tall youth of nearly seventeen. He shook hands all around, and so did the two captains; and then the assistant teacher left the party.

"Oh, it was a shame the way Crabtree treated your brother!" said Captain Harry to Dick. "It's a wonder to me that Captain Putnam keeps him here."

"I was in for getting up a petition to have Crabtree removed," put in Captain Dave. "I think every boy in the academy would sign it."

"I hope Captain Putnam is not so severe," said Fred.

"Not by a jugful, Garrison," came from Captain Harry. "He's strict, and makes everybody toe the mark, but you couldn't find a better all-around man."

"Then he'll suit me."

It was now quite late, and presently a loud, clear bell rang out in the belfry.

"Six o'clock," said Captain Dave Kearney. "That is to bring in the boys from the playground. They have fifteen minutes in which to wash up for supper. Excuse me, I'll be needed in ten minutes to form my company," and soon the newcomers found themselves alone with several others who had just arrived at Putnam Hall.

The cadets were rushing from everywhere to the lavatories, to make themselves presentable on parade. Soon they began to form on the grounds before the building. Dick and the others saw them divide up into two companies, with Harry Blossom at the head of the first and Dave Kearney leading the second. The two companies, called a battalion, were commanded by Major Bart. In addition to the officers, there were two drummers, a bass-drummer, and two fifers.

"Companies, attention!" came the command, and the lines became rigid. "By column of fours—march!" The drums struck up, and away went the columns of each company, to the front of the parade ground. Then they wheeled to the right, the fifers started up a lively air, and the cadets marched around the hall three times, and at last into the door nearest to the mess-hall or dining room.

"By Jinks, that's fine!" cried Sam. "Cadet life will suit me, I'm sure of it."

The cadets had hardly disappeared before one of the waiters in the mess-hall came forward. "Please come right in, gents," he said. "Mr. Strong will give you places at the tables." And they went and soon found themselves seated among as jolly a set of boys as they had ever encountered.

Of course there were exceptions; where would there not be in a crowd of nearly a hundred? There were pupils there who were morose by nature, those who seldom or never smiled, and there were likewise half a dozen of the Dan Baxter order—bullies and worse. We shall see more of all these characters as our tale progresses.

"I wonder if Tom is going to get any supper?" said Dick to his younger brother.

"If they don't give him any, I'll raise a kick, Dick."

"So will I."

"Silence at the table!" came in the sharp tones of Josiah Crabtree, who presided over the particular board at which the Rovers had been placed.

"I was only wondering if my brother was going to get any supper," returned Sam boldly.

"Silence! I will take care of that."

In the midst of the meal a newcomer appeared at the doorway to the messroom. It was Dan Baxter.

"Well, Baxter, how is this?" asked Mr. Strong, the teacher nearest to him.

"I—I was carried to Bar Landing," answered the bully sheepishly.

"Bar Landing? Then you were on the afternoon boat from Ithaca?"

"Yes, sir."

"How did you come to be carried past Cedarville?"

"I—er—fell asleep on the trip."

"Indeed! Well, when next you travel you had better try to keep awake," was George Strong's comment, and a titter passed along the table, which made Dan Baxter very angry.

"Sit down here. Alexander, help Baxter to some supper."

"Yes, sah," came from the waiter; and no more was said. Presently Baxter caught sight of Dick at the table opposite, and he looked daggers at the youth. "He's got it in for me," thought Dick; and he was right.

The supper at an end, the pupils were allowed two hours to themselves— one hour outdoors if they wished it, or both hours in the reading room, which was well supplied with books and all of the best magazines. The newcomers went out in a bunch, and Captain Harry Blossom accompanied them.

"I'll show you the gymnasium, if you wish to see it," he said.

"I would like to know something about Tom," replied Dick. "Where have they placed him?"

"Undoubtedly in the guardroom."

"Where is that?"

"Do you see that window over there?" and Captain Harry pointed with his hand.

"Yes," came from Dick and Sam together.

"Well, that's the window to the place."

"I wonder if I can't talk to my brother?" went on Dick.

"It's against the rules to talk to a prisoner."

"Well, I'm going to talk anyway," said Dick with a recklessness which was unusual to him. "I want to find out just what they are doing with him."

"I guess I had best leave this crowd," remarked the young captain of Company A.

Dick was about to ask why, when Sam nudged him on the arm. "Let him go," whispered the younger brother.

In a moment more Captain Harry had walked away.

"Don't you see what he meant?" asked Sam aloud.

"Well hardly."

"Then you are losing some of your wit, Dick. He didn't want to see us break the rules. I suppose if he had seen us he would have felt it was his duty to report us."

"That's so, Sam. How thick I was! Well, I'm going over to the window now."

"So am I."

"And I'll go too," added Fred.

Off the three hurried across the parade ground, the other new cadets watching them curiously, for all had heard of what Tom had done and how Josiah Crabtree had treated him.

The window of the guardroom was but five feet from the ground. In front of it, however, was an iron fence, placed in the form of a semicircle, at a distance of about ten feet from the opening. The fence was higher than Dick's head, and the iron pickets were sharp-pointed.

"The window to the room is shut," announced the elder Rover, after an inspection in the semi-darkness. "It's a shame, in this warm weather. Poor Tom will be half smothered to death!"

"Wait till I attract his attention," said Sam. Catching up a clod of grass and dirt he threw it against one of the window panes.

A minute of suspense followed, but no face appeared at the window.

"That's queer," said Fred. "It seems to me he would show himself if he was there."

"Perhaps he, can't," said Sam. "He may be chained up in the other end of the room."

"I'm going to make sure," said Dick determinedly. "Sam and Fred, both of you give me a boost up."

"But how will you get back?"

"You can give me another boost through the pickets."

"Hurrah! so we can!" cried Sam. "All right; up you go!"

And up Dick did go, so rapidly that he almost fell over the top of the iron barrier.

"Now, who has a match?" he asked.

"Here you are," said Fred, and passed over several.

Stepping to the window, Dick tapped upon it, and at the same time struck a light, for the room within was pitch-dark. The next instant he muttered a cry of disgust. "Sold!"

"What's that?" came from Sam and Fred.

"The room is empty."

"Then there must be some mistake," said Fred. "Can you see all over inside?"

"Yes."

"Sure Tom isn't asleep in a corner or on a couch—if there is one?" put in Sam. "He would go to sleep if he could."

"He isn't here—no doubt of it," answered Dick, after striking a second match and making another inspection. "Oh!"

Dick blew out the match in a hurry and started back for the fence. He had seen the door of the guardroom open and Josiah Crabtree come in.

The head assistant of Putnam Hall saw the light of the match and by it obtained a good view of Dick's face.

"Ha! that youth has come here to assist his brother to escape!" was the conclusion he reached. He darted for the window and threw it up.

"Come back here, Master Rover!" he cried, as he saw Dick trying to mount the fence.

"Don't you go!" whispered Sam, and tried to assist Dick from the other side, while Fred did the same.

Josiah Crabtree would have leaped from the window, but the bars held him back.

"I'll get you yet!" he ejaculated wrathfully, and, turning, ran from the guardroom, with the intention of capturing Dick on the parade ground.

# CHAPTER IX
## A STRANGE MEETING IN THE WOODS.

To go back to Tom, at the time he was left alone by the head assistant of Putnam Hall, after refusing to give up the keys to his satchel and trunk.

"I've put my foot into it now," thought the boy dismally. "I wonder what Captain Putnam will say to all this when he hears of it? Of course old Crabtree will make out the worst possible case against me."

It was too dark to see much, and he dropped on the couch. He was worried a good deal, yet he was not one to take anything too deeply to heart.

Before long a waiter appeared with a tray containing a big bowl of bread and milk. Had Josiah Crabtree had his own way, he would have sent only bread and water for the lad's supper, but such a proceeding would have been contrary to Captain Putnam's rule. The kind captain realized that his pupils were but boys and should not be treated as real prisoners, even when they did break the academy rules.

"Heah is yo' suppah, sah!" announced Alexander, the waiter, as he set the tray on the table. "Sorry I can't leave the light, sah." He referred to a lamp, also, on the tray, which he now removed.

"What have you got?" asked Tom, sitting up.

"Bowl of bread and milk, sah."

"Is that what they give visitors for supper?"

"Gracious, sah, is yo' a visitah, sah?"

"I consider myself as such until I am placed on the muster roll."

At this Alexander scratched his woolly head. "Well, sah, I don't know nuffin about dat, sah. I has to obey Mr. Crabtree's oahdahs, sah."

"Has Captain Putnam come back yet?"

"No, sah, an' he sent word dat he didn't think he could git back, sah, before morning, sah."

"Humph! Then I'll have to stay here until that time."

"I reckon so, sah."

"It's a jolly shame."

"Dat's right, sah," and Alexander grinned.

"Well, leave the bread and milk. It's better than nothing. But hold on. Who are you?"

"Alexander Pop, sah, at yo' service, sah," and again the colored man grinned. He was a short, fat fellow, the very embodiment of good nature.

"Well, Alexander, if you are at my service, supposing you get me something else to eat beside this bread and milk."

"Oh, sah, I couldn't do dat."

"Yes, you could. Here is a quarter. Don't you want to earn that?" And Tom held out the silver piece.

"Mr. Crabtree would hab me discharged if he cotched me, Master Rober."

"Then don't let him catch you, Aleck, my boy."

At this the negro laughed and showed his immense ivories.

"Yo' is jest de boy I dun like to see, sah," he said. "Jess wait an' I'll do wot I can fo! You but mum's de word, sah-eh?"

"I never peach, Aleck; it's only a coward that does that," concluded Tom.

The negro disappeared from the room, but reappeared in less than ten minutes with something done up in a napkin.

"Dare you am, sah," he said, "two tongue sandwiches and a big piece of layer cake, sah, all I could git, fo' Mrs. Green am werry sharp. And here is a bit of candle, sah, for a light. But please don't let 'em know I brought yo' de things, sah."

"Never a word, Aleck, thank you," answered Tom, and handed over the quarter.

Left again to himself, Tom lost no time in making way, not only with the sandwiches and cake, but also some of the bread and milk, for his day's traveling had left him tremendously hungry. The bit of candle was less than two inches long, and began to splutter just as the meal was finished.

A rattle at the door caused the lad to sweep the cake crumbs out of sight, blow out the candle, and pocket the tiny bit left. Then the light of a lamp lit up the guardroom, and Josiah Crabtree came in.

"Well, Rover, have you enjoyed your supper?" he asked coldly, as he glanced at the half empty bowl.

"Very much," was the youth's equally cold reply.

"You like bread and milk, then," was Crabtree's sarcastic rejoinder.

"Nothing better, sir, for supper."

The head assistant bit his lip, and then set down the lamp.

"Rover, don't you think, you are making a bad beginning?" he said after a pause.

"I don't understand you, Mr. Crabtree."

"Any other boy on joining a school would wish to make his entrance as creditable as possible."

"But I haven't joined this school yet."

"I won't argue that point."

"I wasn't even on your grounds, but in the public highway—and there shot off—what? A simple firecracker. And for that you hauled me to this place, and treat me like one who has broken half the laws of the land. If Captain Putnam upholds you in this matter, do you know what I shall do?"

"Make an additional fool of yourself, I presume."

"I shall write home to my guardian that I do not consider Putnam Hall a proper boarding academy for any boy, and that I want to be put somewhere else."

At these outspoken words Josiah Crabtree grew pale. His great unpopularity was already having its effect upon Captain Putnam, and he was afraid that if he should be the means of losing a pupil it might cost him his place, as much as he knew that the captain did not favor changes in his staff of instructors.

"Don't be unreasonable, my lad," he said, but his tone was much milder than before.

"I don't think I am unreasonable."

"The road is one belonging to this institution—in brief, a private road. You became a pupil here when you entered our carriage, that, which brought you here."

"Does everybody who rides in that carriage become a Putnam Hall pupil?" demanded Tom.

He saw that he was worrying Crabtree, and resolved to keep it up.

"Well—er—we won't argue that point."

"Then supposing we don't argue anything until Captain Putnam comes back? In the meantime if you will release me I'll go to Cedarville and put up at the hotel for the night."

"I shall not release you."

"All right, then. But if my guardian takes me away, mark my words, you shall stand a personal lawsuit for having locked me up here without having any right to do so."

"Why—er—this to me—me, the head assistant here?" screamed Josiah Crabtree.

In his rage he ran over to Tom and caught him by the ear.

He had scarcely done so than Tom put out one foot, gave the teacher a shove, and down went Crabtree flat on his back.

"You villain!" gasped the head assistant, as he scrambled to his feet.

"Don't you pinch my ear again," retorted Tom.

The door was open, and before Crabtree could stop him he ran out into the hallway.

"Hold on!"

"Not much!"

"It will be the worse for you!"

"I'll risk that."

"Stop him, somebody!" screamed Josiah Crabtree at the top of his voice.

Without waiting, Tom ran down the hallway. He knew not where he was going, and, coming, to a door, slipped through. He now found himself in the rear of the Hall and a few seconds later ran across the back garden and dove into the farm lands.

"Free once more," he thought. "And I shan't go back until I am certain Captain Putnam is on hand to receive me. I wonder how Dick and Sam are faring?"

Thinking that his brothers would soon learn of his escape, and not wishing to be caught, he hurried on until the farm lands were passed and he found himself in a woods.

"I'll sweep around in a circle and make for that road leading to Cedarville," he concluded, and trudged on rapidly, for the woods were dark and lonely and not particularly to his liking.

Tom had covered the best part of half a mile: when he saw a light ahead. At first he thought it must shine from the window of some farmhouse, but soon made it out to be from a campfire, situated in something of a hollow and not far from a spring.

"Hullo! Tramps or charcoal burners," he thought. "I wonder if they would be friendly?"

He slackened his pace and approached cautiously until within ten yards of where two men sat in earnest conversation. One man was tall and thin and had a scar on his chin. The other fellow was the thief who had robbed Dick of his watch. At first Tom was not inclined to believe the evidence of his eyesight.

"Perhaps I'm mistaken," he mused.

He resolved to draw nearer and hear if possible what the two men were saying.

A clump of bushes grew close to the spring before mentioned, and he crawled up behind this, thus getting within fifteen feet of the campfire.

"You are certain you saw the boys, Buddy?" he heard the tall man with the scar say.

"I'm as sure of it as I'm sure your name is Arnold Baxt—"

"Hush, Buddy, how many times must I tell you that I want that name dropped, especially around here?"

"There ain't anybody around here to hear us!"

"Well, I don't want the name mentioned. I call you Buddy. You must call me Nolly."

"All right, Nolly."

"Now, you are dead sure you saw the boys on their way to Putnam Hall?"

"I am."

"How much have you drank today?"

"Only two glasses, this morning. Oh, it was them," went on Buddy, with a total disregard for grammar.

The tall man muttered something under his breath.

"It's too bad," he said aloud.

"What's too bad?"

"That they are going to Putnam Hall. Still, I don't know as it will amount to anything. But I reckon you had best get out of the neighborhood."

"I'm going to get out."

"What brought you here?"

"I wanted to see you again, as I said before."

"About what?"

"That mining deal."

"I can't do anything at present."

"Why not?"

"There are some papers missing, Buddy. As soon as I get those I'll be in a condition to go ahead. You know, I've got to move slowly."

"Well, what brought you here?"

"That is my business."

"Every few months or so you come up to Cedarville, Baxt—— Nolly, and on a secret mission."

"Well, who has a better right? Come, let us talk about something else. If you— Hullo, what's that?"

Both men leaped to their feet as a sound from the bushes back of the spring reached their ears.

Tom had been lying as quiet as a mouse when a pinching-bug, as they are commonly called, had dropped from one of the bushes onto his neck.

The bug was as big as a walnut shell, and had fine nippers, and when he took hold of the skin Tom could not help but make a slight noise as he tried to throw the bug off.

Before the boy could arise to his feet the two men were rushing upon him, Buddy with a stick and the tall man with something which he had drawn from his pocket. It was a sand-bag, a favorite weapon used in our large cities by footpads.

# CHAPTER X
## SETTLING DOWN AT THE HALL

"It's a boy!" cried the tall, slim man.

"One of the boys!" came from the tramp known as Buddy.

"You don't say!" The tall man turned to Tom. "How did you get here?"

"Walked," answered Tom as calmly as he could, although this is not saying much, for he realized that the pair before him were desperate characters and that he was no match for them.

"Have you been spying on us?" demanded the fellow called Nolly.

"I've been spying on this man," answered Tom, pointing to the other fellow. "He stole my brother's watch. What have you done with it?"

"Never stole a watch in me life!" returned Buddy quickly.

"I say you did, and it will do no good to deny it."

"If you say I stole any watch I'll—I'll knock yer down," cried Buddy fiercely.

And he rushed at Tom and aimed a blow at the boy's head with his stick.

Nolly also ran forward with his sand-bag; and seeing this, Tom leaped back, and was soon making tracks as fast as his legs could carry him.

The two men did not pursue him far. Instead, they turned and ran in the opposite direction.

Tom hurried on until he came within sight of a large farmhouse. Reaching the front door, he used the brass knocker vigorously.

Soon an upper window was raised, and the head of a middle-aged man was thrust out.

"Who is there?" he demanded.

"I want help, sir," answered Tom. "I am a pupil at Putnam Hall, and I have just spotted a fellow in this neighborhood who robbed my brother of a gold watch."

"Is that so!"

"Oh, papa, is it one of the boys Grace and I were telling you about?" came in the voice of Nellie Laning. "Aren't you Tom Rover?"

"Yes. This must be Mr. Laning."

"Yes, my boy, I am John Laning," answered the farmer. "I will be down in a moment. We are in the habit of retiring early."

In a few minutes Tom was let into the house, and he told his story to John Laning, his wife, and the two girls, all of whom listened with interest.

Then a hired man was aroused, and the two men and the boy hurried to where the campfire had been located.

But, as stated before, Buddy and Nolly had made good use of their time, and no trace of them was to be found.

"They have skipped out," said Mr. Laning.

"To look for them will be worse than looking for spiders in a corn stack. I suppose you'll be getting back to Putnam Hall now?"

"If it is all the same, I would like to engage a room at your farmhouse for the night," answered Tom, and told his tale.

At the mention of Josiah Crabtree's name John Laning's face grew dark.

"I don't wonder you had a row with that man," he said. "I know him only too well. You can stay at my house if you will, and it shall not cost you a cent."

"Hullo, here is luck!" thought Tom, and thanked the farmer for his offer.

When they got back to the farmhouse Tom's story had to be told to Grace and Nellie, while Mr. Laning went off to prepare a room for the youth.

"Oh, Josiah Crabtree!" cried Nelly. "Why, don't you know he is trying to court our Aunt Lucy?"

"Your Aunt Lucy? Who is she?"

"Dora Stanhope's mother. Dora's father is dead, you know."

"Great Caesar!" burst from Tom; "I hope Dora never gets him for a stepfather!"

"So do all of us, Tom; but I'm afraid he has made quite an impression on Aunt Lucy. She is rich; and my own idea is that Josiah Crabtree is after her money."

"He's none too good for it," was Tom's blunt comment.

The girls and the lad chatted together for half an hour, and then all retired for the balance of the night.

"They're awfully sweet," thought the boy, "these two, and Dora too."

He slept soundly, and did not arise until after seven. On coming below he found a hot breakfast awaiting him, to which it is perhaps needless to state he did full justice.

While he was talking to the girls, and finishing up at the same time, Mr. Laning came in.

"Thought I would tell you that Captain Putnam just drove down the Hall road on his way to the school," he announced.

"Then I'll get back at once," said Tom, and bade the various members of the family good-by. "Hope we meet again soon," he whispered to the girls, and this made both blush.

Mr. Laning would have driven the lad to the academy, but Tom declined the offer and set off on foot. It did not take him long to cover the distance, and he entered the grounds as unconcernedly as though nothing out of the ordinary had happened.

"Hullo!" cried several cadets as they noticed him. "Where did you come from? Mr. Crabtree has been looking all over for you."

"I don't wish to see him. I wish to see Captain Putnam? Where is he?"

"Gracious, but you're a cool one!" remarked one of the cadets. "The captain is in his office, I think."

"Will you please show me to the place?"

"Certainly."

The office was a finely furnished apartment just off the main classroom. Tom knocked on the door.

"Come in," said a cheery voice, and the boy calmly entered to find himself confronted not only by Captain Putnam, but likewise by Josiah Crabtree.

"Ah! Here is the young reprobate now!" cried Crabtree, as rushing up, he grasped Tom by the arm.

"You will kindly let go of my arm, Mr. Crabtree," said Tom steadily.

"You shan't run away again!"

"That's true—now Captain Putnam is here."

"So this is Thomas Rover," said Captain Victor Putnam, with something like a twinkle in his clear eyes. "Rover, I have heard a rather serious report about you and your brother Richard."

"What kind of a report, if I may ask, sir?"

"Mr. Crabtree says you have been impudent to him, and that when he locked you in the guardroom for breaking the rules you attacked him and knocked him down."

"He attacked me first. If anybody attacked you, wouldn't you be apt to knock him down if you could?"

"That would depend upon, circumstances, Rover. If a man attacked me on the street I would certainly endeavor to defend myself to the best of my ability. But you must remember that you are a pupil here, and Mr. Crabtree is one of your masters, appointed by me."

"I am not a pupil yet, sir—although I hope to be very soon."

"Why, what do you mean?" demanded Victor Putnam, and now his voice grew stern. Many a boy would have flinched, but Tom had determined to say just what he thought of Crabtree, and he stood his ground.

"I mean just this, Captain Putnam. I came to Putnam Hall with the best intention in the world of doing my duty as a pupil and becoming a credit to your institution. I hadn't a thought of breaking a rule or being impudent. Before I entered your grounds I thought of a big fire cracker I had in my pocket, and just for the fun of the thing set the cracker off, as a sort of farewell to the outdoor life so soon to be left behind."

"Captain Putnam, are you going to listen to such tomfoolery?" interrupted Josiah Crabtree.

"I believe I have a right to tell my story," answered Tom. "Unless that right is granted, I shall leave the Hall, go back to my guardian, and tell him that I refuse to become a pupil here."

"You are a pupil already," snarled Crabtree.

"I am not—and that is just the point I am trying to make," went on Tom to the owner of Putnam Hall. "As soon as the firecracker went off, this man rushed up and demanded an explanation. He was going to lock up my brother first, but I said I had fired the cracker, and so he compelled me to go to the guardroom with him. I was locked in and treated to bread and milk for supper, and he wanted to steal the keys of my trunk and valise from me."

"Steal!" ejaculated Josiah Crabtree.

"That is what it amounted to, for the keys, and boxes are my property."

"Mr. Crabtree merely wanted to see that your baggage contained nothing improper," put in Captain Putnam. "There are certain things we do not allow boys to bring into the institution."

"Then he had a right to keep my baggage out until I was properly enrolled as a pupil. I did not bring in the trunk and bag myself."

At this Captain Putnam began to smile.

"I see the point you are trying to make, Rover. You are trying to prove that you were placed under arrest, so to speak, before you were under our authority here."

"Exactly. I will leave it to you, Captain Putnam, if I was really a pupil when Mr. Crabtree hauled me off to the guardroom."

At this plain question the face of the owner of the Hall became a study.

"You make a very fine distinction, Rover," he answered slowly.

"Perhaps so, sir; and I do it because I want to begin right here. If I am to be handicapped at the start of my career, what is the use of my trying to make a record for myself?" and Tom looked the master of Putnam Hall full in the face.

Without a word Captain Putnam held out his hand. "Thomas, you have considerable spirit, but I think your heart is in the right place, and I am willing to try you. Supposing you enroll as a pupil now, and we let bygones be bygones?"

"With all my heart, sir!" cried Tom, glad to have the whole affair settled so easily.

"Why, are you going to let the—the young rascal go?" demanded Josiah Crabtree, in amazement.

"I'm not a rascal, Mr. Crabtree."

"Yes, you are!"

"Mr. Crabtree, I have decided to drop the matter," put in Captain Putnam, in a tone which admitted of no dispute, and the head assistant fell back abashed. "Rover says he wishes to make a record for himself, and I am inclined to help him. He starts his term free and clear of all charges against him—and his brother whom you have locked up shall do likewise. Kindly call Mr. Strong."

"It is a—a most unusual proceeding," growled the head assistant.

"Perhaps, but we will talk that matter over at another time."

Josiah Crabtree went out; and in a minute George Strong appeared, and Tom was turned over to him, to sign the roll of the academy and to join Sam, Fred, and the others in the class room over which Mr. Strong presided.

"Hullo, you're back," whispered Sam, but no more could be said until recess, when Tom told his story in detail. In the meantime Dick was released.

"So you met the fellow who stole my watch!" cried the elder brother. "I wish you had got the timepiece."

"So do I, Dick."

Dick had been captured by Josiah Crabtree just as he was vaulting the iron fence around the guardroom window. The head assistant had locked him up in the apartment Tom had occupied, and there Dick had remained all night.

"Oh, Crabtree is a terror!" said Dick later on. "I hope Dora Stanhope's mother never marries him."

"I'll wager neither of you have heard the last of Crabtree, even if we are not in his classes," remarked Sam. "He will watch for a chance to get even, mark my words."

"I don't doubt it, Sam," answered Tom. "But let him come on. I intend to do my duty as a cadet, and I am not afraid of him."

# CHAPTER XI
# A ROW IN THE GYMNASIUM

For several days matters moved along smoothly with the Rover boys. In that time their chums, Frank Harrington and Larry Colby, arrived, and these, with Fred, made up the "Metropolitan Sextet," as they called themselves—the sole occupants of dormitory No. 6.

Next to this dormitory was apartment five, occupied by Dan Baxter, Mumps, and six others of the bully's cronies. The two apartments were connected by a door, but this was nailed up.

So far there had been no open rupture between Baxter and Dick, but there was trouble "in the air," and it was bound to reach a climax sooner or later.

Fortunately for Dick and his brothers, Captain Putnam had cadet uniforms to fit them, and the three were now dressed in true military style. The other boys had to wait until uniforms could be made for them.

The first day at Putnam Hall was spent in assigning the newcomers to the various classes, according to their knowledge. On the second day the three Rover boys were placed in the awkward squad, to learn the military drill.

The squad was presided over by Corporal Mark King, a youth who was cut out to be a soldier, although his father was a sea captain.

"Now then, line up!" he called out to the newcomers. "All of you will please toe that crack in the floor; now turn out your toes like this, and put your shoulders back, hands with the palms to the front."

His instructions were followed to the letter, for all were anxious to learn as fast as possible.

"Now the first thing to remember is to say nothing, but obey orders promptly," exclaimed the corporal. "When an order is given the first part is a warning, while the conclusion is the time when that order must be executed. For, instance, I tell you 'Eyes right!' I say 'Eyes,' and you get ready to move your eyes; I add 'Right,' and you instantly turn them to the right, and keep them there. Now we'll try. Eyes—right! Great smoke! number four, you turned them to the left! Now again: Eyes—right! Good! Eyes—front! That's first-class. Now: Eyes—left! Eyes—front! That couldn't be better."

And so it went on for an hour, during which the boys learned not alone how to use their eyes, but also to "left face," "right face," "front face," and "about face"—that is, to turn directly to the rear. Then they learned how to mark time "with their feet, starting with the left foot."

"Tomorrow you shall learn how to march," said Corporal King when the drilling was over. "And then each of you will get a gun and go through the manual of arms."

"Will we learn how to shoot?" asked Tom. "I can shoot a little already."

"We have target practice once a month, and during the annual encampment," concluded the corporal.

"I wish that encampment was already at hand!" sighed Sam. He imagined that life under a tent would just suit him.

As soon as the boys "got the run" of the institution they began to feel at home. They made friends rapidly, especially when it became known that Sam was a fine runner and Tom a capital baseball player. There were several baseball teams in the school, and they frequently played matches on Saturday afternoons.

The gymnasium pleased Dick as much as it did his younger brothers, and nearly every day, he spent a quarter of an hour or more in the building, using one apparatus or another, for the building was fitted up with rings, parallel bars, wooden horses, pulling machines, and other paraphernalia of athletic usage.

One afternoon Dick had just begun to use a set of parallel bars when Dan Baxter sauntered in, accompanied by Mumps and two other cronies.

There were very few cadets in the building at the time, and Baxter came directly to Dick.

"I guess we can settle that little affair now," muttered the bully, and slapped Dick on the cheek. "That for interfering with my doing on the boat."

Being on the bars, Dick could not ward off the blow, but he immediately sprang down, and with flushed cheeks leaped in front of Baxter.

"You seem very anxious to fight," he said in a low, steady voice. "You can, therefore, take that for a starter!" And hauling off with his right fist, he struck Dan Baxter fairly and squarely upon the nose, causing the blood to spurt and sending the bully to the floor like a shot.

If ever there was an individual taken by surprise it was the bully of Putnam Hall. He had not anticipated such a sudden and determined resistance, and for several seconds he lay still, too dazed to move. In the meantime his friends sprang forward, but Dick waved them off.

"My fight is with Baxter," he said. "I want you to keep your hands out of it."

"You hit him when he wasn't prepared," blustered Mumps.

"And he hit me when I was not prepared. Stand back!"

And Dick made such a show of being ready to attack Mumps that the toady fell back in great alarm.

In the meanwhile Dan Baxter arose, and tried to stop the flow of blood with his handkerchief. "I'll get even with you, Rover!" he growled behind the stained cloth.

"At any time you please, Baxter," returned Dick. "But don't you take me off my guard again, or I'll have no mercy on you."

"Do you dare to meet me in a fair, standing up fight?" demanded the bully.

"I certainly do."

"All right, then. Next Saturday afternoon at three."

Dick bowed. "Where?" he questioned.

"In the patch of woods behind the cornfield."

"All right."

"Mums is the word, fellows," said Baxter to his cronies. "You will keep this to yourself, Rover, won't you?"

"How many do you expect to bring to the fight?"

"Only the four fellows who are here."

"Very well; I will bring a like number."

"Want to tell everybody, don't you?"

"No, but I think I am entitled to fair play; and that means that I must have as many friends there as you have."

"All right," grumbled Baxter, but he evidently did not like the arrangement. A moment later he hurried off, to do what he could to prevent his nose from swelling.

Dick told only his brothers and his chums of what had occurred, but the news leaked out that a fight was on, and Saturday afternoon found at least twenty cadets in the secret and on their way to witness the "mill," as those who had read something about prize-fighting were wont to call the contest.

Now, lest my readers obtain a false impression of my views on this subject, let me state plainly that I do not believe in fights, between boys or otherwise. They are brutal, far from manly, and add nothing to the strength of one's character. It is well enough to know how to defend one's self when occasion requires, but such occasions occur but rarely.

But I have set out to relate the adventures of the Rover boys, in school and out, and on land and sea, and I feel I must be truthful and tell everything just as it happened, not only in this volume, but in all those which are to follow; and, consequently, I shall tell of the fight as the particulars were related to me by Sam Rover, Fred Garrison and others—details which I am certain are correct.

The spot was a sheltered one, and on the edge of the woods two spies were posted, to warn the contestants should Josiah Crabtree or any of the other teachers appear, for fighting was against the rules of Putnam Hall, and neither Dick nor Baxter wanted to be caught.

Both came to the spot promptly, and, without preliminary talking, took off their coats, collars, ties, and caps. A ring was formed, and Dick stepped forward and faced Baxter.

The bully was several inches taller than his opponent and at least fifteen pounds heavier. His nose was a bit swollen, and there was a sneer upon his coarse face.

"Rover, if you wish to apologize to me you can do so, and save yourself a thrashing," he remarked.

"I can take care of myself, Baxter. Perhaps you would like me to make a similar proposition to you. If so, let me say it is too late; I came here to give you a well-deserved thrashing, and I mean to stick to my determination."

"Phew, but we talk big!" muttered Mumps.

"You keep your oar out, Mumps," put in Tom. "If you don't I'll give you a hiding, just as soon as Dick is done with Dan."

"Will you? Maybe you'll be the one to catch it," muttered Mumps. Nevertheless, he said no more.

"Are you ready?" asked the boy who acted as timekeeper.

"I am," said Dick.

"So am I," returned Baxter, and hurled himself at his opponent without a second's delay.

He had expected to catch Dick napping, but he found himself mistaken. A blow aimed at Dick's face was well parried, and in return Dick hit Baxter heavily on the shoulder.

"Hurrah! Score one for Dick!" cried Larry Colby. "That's right, old man, keep at him."

"Keep cool, Dan!" put in Mumps. "You can polish him off at your leisure."

The blow on the shoulder staggered Baxter, and he fell back, to become more cautious; and then the two boys began to circle around and around, each looking for a favorable "opening." At last Baxter thought he saw what he wanted, and struck out again, and Dick was hit on the cheek.

"That's the way, Baxter!" came the cry.

"That was a teaser! Give him another!"

Again Baxter launched out, and now Dick was hit on the arm. He slipped to one side, and struck out like lightning, and the bully caught it in the neck, something which, spun him around like a top.

"Another for Dick!" cried Frank Harrington. "Keep it up!"

Again the two boys faced each other. But only for an instant. With a savage cry Baxter sprang upon Dick as if to fairly tear him apart. One blow landed upon Dick's arm and a second on his chest.

"It's Baxter's fight! Baxter is still king of this school!"

"You might as well give it up, Rover; he's too many for you!"

So the cries ran on, while the bully, encouraged by his success, renewed his efforts; and an additional blow sent Dick to the ground in a heap.

# CHAPTER XII
## FAIR AND FOUL FIGHTING

As Dick went down, Tom and Sam uttered cries of chagrin and horror. The eldest Rover had been struck on the chin, and the blood was flowing from a deep scratch.

"Get up! Get up, Dick!" cried Tom. "Don't say you are beaten!"

"Yes, yes; get up and go at him!" added Sam.

The urging was unnecessary, as Dick was already scrambling up. Dan Baxter made a dash at him, intending to strike him while he was down, but a fierce look from Tom stopped him.

"You'll fight fair, Baxter," were Tom's words.

"Yes, he'll fight fair," repeated Dick, throwing back his head as if to collect himself. "Fellow-students, Dan Baxter is not fit to be a pupil at this academy."

"Why not?" came in a chorus.

"He is not fighting me fairly."

"What do you mean?" blustered Mumps.

"Don't find fault because he knocked you down," added another of the bully's cronies.

"I say he is not fighting fair," repeated Dick stoutly. "He has something in each hand."

At this unexpected announcement Dan Baxter started back and changed color. Then of a sudden he placed both hands into his trouser pockets.

"He is putting the things out of sight!" cried Tom, who saw through the bully's intentions.

"Come, Baxter, show us what you had."

"I didn't have anything," growled the bully. "If you say I had I'll punch your head off. This is only a ruse to, let Dick gain time to get his wind."

"That's it!" cried Mumps. "Go at him, Dan, and finish him!"

"Baxter daren't turn out his pockets," said Sam, "Do it if you dare."

"There is what I have in them," answered the bully, pulling a trunk key from one pocket and some small change from the other. "Perhaps you'll say I was fighting with these in my hands."

"Turn the pockets, out!" demanded Dick.

"Yes, turn 'em out!" added Fred, and a dozen others took up the cry.

"I won't do it," growled Baxter, but it was plain to see that he was growing uneasy. "I'm a gentleman, and I can whip Rover with ease, and do it fairly, too!"

While he was speaking Larry Colby had come up behind him. Ere Baxter could stop the movement, Larry pushed his hand into one of the bully's pockets and turned it out. A jagged stone as big as a walnut dropped to the ground.

"There, see that!" cried Larry. "For shame, Baxter!"

"I didn't have the stone—you placed it there!" blustered the so-styled king of the school.

"Didn't you though?" said Fred Garrison, who had also come up behind Baxter, and he quickly hauled another stone from the other pocket.

"That is how he scratched me," said Dick. "I was sure he had something in his hand."

"It's a put-up job!" howled Baxter, growing red in the face. "If you want to continue the fight, come on!" and he squared off again.

"That's the talk!" said Mumps. "Let both show their hands! Perhaps Rover has some stones, too!"

Both opened their palms, then doubled up their fists. Baxter was the first to strike out. But, as quick as lightning, Dick dodged the blow and landed vigorously upon the bully's chest. Before Baxter could recover, Dick struck out again, and the bully caught it straight in the left eye.

"Oh!" he yelled in pain, and put his hand up to the injured optic, which began to grow black rapidly. Then he struck out wildly half a dozen times. He was growing excited, while Dick was as calm as ever. Watching his opportunity, Dick struck out with all his force, and Baxter received a crack on the nose which caused him to fall back into the arms of Mumps. As that nose had been struck heavily in the gymnasium, it was decidedly tender, and Baxter roared with pain.

"Have you had enough?" demanded Dick, coming up to him.

Yes—Baxter had had more than enough; but he did not wish to acknowledge it. He made a sign to Mumps previously agreed upon, and Mumps raised his cap as a signal to one of the spies set on guard.

"Stop the fight!" cried the guard instantly. "Somebody is coming!"

"Nonsense—nobody is coming!" said the other spy, but Baxter would not listen to him.

"I'm not going to be caught—I'll finish this some other time," he said to Dick, and hurried away with Mumps and his other friends, leaving Dick the victor beyond question.

"I knew you could do it!" cried Tom, as he fairly hugged his elder brother.

"I'll wager he won't bother you again."

"No, indeed!" put in Sam; and Fred and the others said the same. That was the first and last time that Dan Baxter fought any of the boys openly, but he was their bitter enemy in secret; we shall learn in this and other volumes.

As soon as Baxter had retreated, Dick and his brothers hurried to a nearby brook, where the elder Rover took a wash, and tried by other means to remove the traces of the contest from his person. He had a slight swelling on the scratched chin, but that was all, and inside of an hour felt quite like himself once more.

With Baxter it was very different, and the Sunday following he asked to be excused from attending church services in the Hall, saying he had fallen on some rocks and hurt his face. On hearing this, Captain Putnam came to see him.

"Sorry to hear this, Baxter," he said. "Do you think you need a doctor?"

"No, sir; I'll be all right in a few days."

"Where did you fall?"

"Down by the brook, while we were playing tag."

"Indeed! Well, you want to be more careful in the future," was Captain Putnam's advice, and then he left Baxter. If he suspected anything he did not let on. To a certain extent he believed in letting boys fight out their own battles.

The Rover boys had come to Putnam Hall in the fall, and now summer sports were cast aside among the pupils, and football and hare and hounds became the rage.

As we know, Sam was an excellent runner, and hare and hounds just suited him.

"We must ask the captain to let us take a long trip next Saturday afternoon," he said; and the boys went to the owner of Putnam Hall in a body and obtained permission.

It was decided that Sam and Fred should be the hares, while Larry Colby was to be leading hound. As Frank Harrington had a trumpet he was made whipper-in. Captain Putnam supplied the boys with a package of old copying books, and these were cut up into small bits and stuffed into two pillow cases loaned by Mrs. Green.

The start was made on a clear but frosty afternoon. The hares stood on the parade ground, with the hounds, to the number of thirty, behind them. George Strong had consented to start them off. The hares were to be given three minutes start of the little scholars and five minutes start of the big boys.

"All ready?" asked the second assistant of Putnam Hall, as he took out his watch.

"All ready," answered Sam and Fred.

"Then go!" And away went the two boys straight for the cornfield, dropping bits of paper as they sped along. They leaped the fence in the rear, crossed the brook, and then started along a path leading through the woods beyond.

"We mustn't dream of letting them catch us," remarked Sam, as he ran on, with Fred directly behind him. "I wonder where this path leads to?"

"The top of the mountain, so Mr. Strong told me. He said there was another path coming down to the westward."

On and on they went along the path until they came to a narrow mountain road. Here they met a farmer carting a number of logs in his wagon, and stopped him to ask a few questions.

"Yes, that road will take you right up to the top," he said. "But you want to be careful and not make a wrong turn, or you may get lost."

"I'm not afraid of being lost," said Fred with a light laugh; and on they sped again, as rapidly as ever, for Fred was as good a runner as Sam, and the pair worked very well together.

At the top of the first rise of ground they came to a spot that was somewhat bare, and here they halted to look back.

"There are the small fellows!" cried Sam, pointing with his finger. "And the big ones are not far behind."

"They are speeding along in good shape," was Fred's comment. "Come on, before they spot us!" And they hurried up the next hill. Here they encountered a number of rocks, and were brought to a halt several times to determine which was the best path to pursue.

"By jinks! the farmer was right—we are getting lost!" said Sam presently.

"Where is the path?"

"I think it is to the right."

"And I think it is to the left."

At this both lads looked at each other, then burst out laughing.

"It can't be in both directions, Fred."

"That's true, and I am sure I am right."

"All right, we'll try it," and they did, but it was a good ten minutes before the path came into view again, and meanwhile the first of the hounds drew dangerously close.

But the game was by no means over, as we shall see.

# CHAPTER XIII
## WHAT THE GAME OF HARE AND HOUND LED TO

"What a glorious view!"

It was Sam who uttered the words. The top of the mountain had been reached at last, and the boys were feasting their eyes on the grand panorama spread on all sides.

"How beautiful the lake looks!" said Fred.

"And how far one can see!"

"It's a pity we didn't bring a pair of glasses with us, Fred. But, say, I'm hungry."

"So am I. Let us eat that lunch at once and then start on the return."

Each had brought a sandwich along, and these were soon consumed and washed down with a drink of cold water from a spring not far away. Then on they went, over the top of the mountain, and along a path which they thought would bring them around its western base. It was now four o'clock, leaving them two hours in which to get back to Putnam Hall.

About a third of the distance down the mountain side had been covered, and Sam was slightly in advance, when suddenly he uttered a cry of alarm.

"Look out, Fred!"

"What is it?"

"A snake!"

"Where?"

"Over yonder! And he is coming for us!"

Sam was right; it was a snake—an angry looking reptile all of six feet long, and as thick as Sam's wrist. It hissed savagely as it advanced, first upon Sam and then upon Fred.

If there was one thing which could fill Fred Garrison full of terror it was a snake, and the yell he gave would have outmatched that of an Indian on the warpath.

"Save me!" he screamed. "Don't let him touch me!" "Jump back!" cried Sam, and leaped himself. Then, seeing a tall rock handy, he sprang upon it, and here Fred joined him.

Now, it happened that the snake had its home under the rock, and the movement of the lads made it more angry than ever. With a fierce hiss it came for the rock and disappeared underneath, out of the range of their vision.

"It's gone under the rock!" panted Fred. He was so agitated he could scarcely speak.

"I know it," returned Sam. "I wonder if it means to crawl up here?"

"Oh, don't say that, Sam. I—I—can't we hit it with something?"

"I haven't a thing but the bag of paper."

"Neither have I. Oh, what shall we do?"

"Perhaps, we had better stay here until the others come up."

"Do you think the snake will keep quiet that long?"

"I'm sure I don't know."

Very much disturbed, the two boys peered over the edge of the rock. They were not versed in the different species of reptiles, and knew not but that the one at hand might be poisonous.

"I see his tail!" cried Fred with a shiver.

"He is moving around as if getting ready to come out."

"I wonder if I can grab him by the tail?" mused Sam.

"Grab him? Oh Sam!"

"I've heard you can catch them by the tail, snap them, and make their heads fly right off."

"Gracious, I wouldn't attempt it!"

While Fred was speaking the tail of the snake came up on the side of the rock. Setting his teeth, Sam bent down and made a reach for the slippery thing, and caught it tight.

With a hiss the snake raised its head, its diamond-like eyes shining like twin stars.

"You'll be poisoned!" shrieked Fred, when whack! Sam gave the body of the reptile a swing and brought the head down with great force on the edge of the rock.

One blow was enough, for the head was mashed flat. Then Sam threw the body into the bushes, there to quiver and twist for several hours to come, although life was extinct.

Fred was as white as a sheet as he leaped to the ground. "I couldn't have done that for a million dollars!" he declared. "What a splendid nerve you have, Sam."

"My father told me how to catch a snake in that way," exclaimed Sam. "But hurry, or the hounds will overtake us. I can hear them coming."

"Your father must have been equally brave, then," answered Fred, as they started off on, a run. "By the way, have you heard anything of him yet?"

"Not a word, Fred."

"Don't it make you feel bad at times?"

"Does it, Fred! Why, some nights I can't go to sleep for thinking of where he may be—dead in the heart of Africa, or perhaps a captive of some savage tribe."

"Have they ever hunted for him?"

"Several have gone out, but no traces are to be had. Dick, Tom, and I are in to hunt for him, though, as soon as our Uncle Randolph will permit it."

"That's an idea. But you may have to go right into the jungles for him."

"I don't care if we have to go to the top of the North Pole, if only we find him," answered Sam with quiet determination.

Inside of half an hour the bottom of the mountain was gained, and then they struck out along a road which presently took them within sight of the Stanhope homestead.

"I wonder if we have time to call on Dora?" mused Fred. "It would be a scheme to leave our paper trail right through their garden."

"Glorious!" burst from Sam, caught by the idea. "I am certain Dora Stanhope will appreciate the sport."

It did not take them long to reach the garden around the farmhouse; and, running up the path, they ascended a side porch.

As they did so two forms appeared around the house. One was Mrs. Stanhope, wearing a shawl over her shoulders and a bonnet on her head, and the second was Josiah Crabtree!

"Old Crabtree!" murmured Sam, and then of a sudden he pulled Fred out of sight behind some lattice-work inclosing one end of the porch.

"We must hurry, my dear, or we may be too late," Josiah Crabtree was saying; and now the boys noted that he was conducting the lady toward a carriage standing by the horse block.

"I—I—had we not better wait until next week, Josiah?" questioned Mrs. Stanhope timidly. She was a pale, delicate woman of forty, of a shrinking nature, easily led by others.

"No, my dear, there is no use in waiting."

"But Dora—?"

"You must not mind what your daughter says, my dear. When we are married she will easily become reconciled to the change, mark my words."

"Gracious, old Crabtree is going to marry her!" whispered Sam. "Poor Dora!"

"She wants me to wait," continued the lady.

"And you ought to wait, mother," came in Dora's voice; and now she too came into sight, but without a hat or wraps.

"Mr. Crabtree wishes very much to have the ceremony performed this afternoon, Dora dear."

"If he wants to marry you, why can't he do it openly—at home or in our church?"

"He is averse to any display."

"It seems to me it is a very sneaking way to do," answered Dora coldly. "When you and papa were married the wedding was well attended, so I have been told."

"Your father and myself are different persons, Miss Dora," interrupted Josiah Crabtree stiffly. "I prefer a quiet wedding, and no time is better than the present. I shall at once resign my position at Putnam Hall and come to live here."

Dora Stanhope's lip curled in scorn. She saw through Josiah Crabtree's motives, even though her mother did not.

"If you wish to marry my mother, why do you not make preparations to support her?" she said.

"Dora!" cried Mrs. Stanhope pleadingly.

"I mean what I say, mother. He intends to marry you and then make you support him, out of the proceeds of this farm."

"You are entirely mistaken," interrupted Josiah Crabtree. "Perhaps you do not know that I am worth, in bank stocks and in bonds, between twenty and thirty thousand dollars."

"I would like to see the stocks and bonds," said the girl.

"So would I," whispered Fred to Sam. "I'll wager he isn't worth a thousand dollars all told although they say he is a good deal of a miser."

"Dora, do not insult Mr. Crabtree. If you wish to come along and see the ceremony performed, put on your things...."

"I do not wish to go."

"Very well, then; you had best return to the house."

"It is a shame!" cried the girl, and burst into tears.

"We will be back by seven o'clock," said Josiah Crabtree, and led the widow down the garden path to where the carriage was standing.

"I wish I could stop this wedding," whispered Sam to his chum.

"I am with you on that," returned Fred.

"Creation, here come the hounds! Just the thing!"

He looked at Sam, and his chum, instantly understood. Leaving the porch at a bound, they ran across the garden.

"Hurrah! we have you!" yelled Larry Colby, as he rushed up, followed by Tom, Dick, and a dozen of the other big cadets.

"Quick, this way!" cried Sam. "Do you see that carriage?"

"Of course we do," answered Tom.

"It contains Mrs. Stanhope and old Crabtree. They are going to drive off and get married against Dora Stanhope's wishes."

"Phew!" came in a low whistle from the eldest of the Rover Boys.

"We ought to stop this affair," went on Fred.

"Old Crabby is going to get married!" came in a shout. "Come on, let us go along!"

And pell-mell went the boys after the carriage, which had just turned from the horse-block with the teacher and Mrs. Stanhope inside, and a farmhand named Borgy on the front seat.

# CHAPTER XIV
# JOSIAH CRABTREE IN DIFFICULTY

Dora Stanhope had witnessed the approach of the boys, and now she came out into the garden again and confronted them. She blushed prettily upon seeing Dick and several others with whom she was acquainted.

"I understand that Mr. Crabtree is about to be married," said Dick in a low tone.

"Yes, he insists on marrying my mother this afternoon. He has been at her about this for several months," answered Dora between her sobs.

"Evidently you oppose the marriage."

"I—I hate Mr. Crabtree!" came almost fiercely. "He is—is nothing like my poor dead papa was."

"I believe you, Dora," answered Dick. "I don't see what your mother can find in him to like. We hate him at the academy."

"I know it—and I imagine Captain Putnam is preparing to get rid of him, for I heard he was corresponding with a teacher in Buffalo—one who has been head master in a military academy out in that vicinity."

"Indeed! I hope we do get clear of him—and I wish you could get clear of him too."

"It doesn't seem as if I could," sighed Dora. "He has wound my mother right around his finger, so to speak. But what are those other boys going to do?" And she pointed to the balance of the cadets, who were following closely upon the wheels of the carriage, which had turned into the highway leading to Cedarville.

"I'll go after them and see," said Dick, and turned to leave. Then he came to a halt and turned back. "Dora, I am awfully sorry for you," he whispered. "If I can ever do anything for you, don't hesitate to call on me."

"I'll remember that, Dick," she replied gratefully, but never dreamed of how much she would one day require his aid.

When Dick joined the crowd he found it on all sides of the carriage, shouting and hurrahing wildly. At first Josiah Crabtree pretended to pay no attention, but presently he spoke to the driver, and the turnout came to a halt.

"Students, what does this unseemly conduct mean?" he demanded harshly.

"Why, Mr. Crabtree, is that you!" exclaimed Frank Harrington in pretended surprise.

"Yes, Harrington. I say, what does it mean?"

"We are out playing hare and hounds, sir."

"But you are following this carriage."

"Oh, no, sir, we are following the paper scent, sir," answered Larry Colby, and pointed to the pieces of paper, which Fred Harrison was slyly dropping just in front of the horses.

"Then our carriage is on the trail," sighed Josiah Crabtree. "It is very annoying."

"Oh, it doesn't bother us much, sir," answered Frank coolly.

"Bother you! It is myself and Mrs. Stanhope to whom I referred. Make the hares take another course."

"Can't do that, sir, until we catch them."

"But why must you keep so close to this carriage?"

"I don't know, sir. Perhaps it is the carriage which is keeping close to us."

Josiah Crabtree looked more angry than ever. He spoke to the driver, with a view to increasing the speed of the team, but Borgy had entered into the spirit of the fun at hand, and he was, moreover, a great friend of Dora, and he shook his head. "Couldn't do it sir," he said. "I wouldn't want to run the risk of winding them."

"Do you mean to say they cannot outrun these boys?" demanded the head assistant at Putnam Hall.

"Hardly, sir—the lads is uncommonly good runners," answered Borgy meekly.

"I will show you how to manage them!" ejaculated Josiah Crabtree, and stepped over to the front seat.

"Oh, Josiah, be careful!" pleaded Mrs. Stanhope.

"I know how to drive horses, so don't worry," answered Crabtree, and took up both reins and whip. Before Borgy could stop him he had given one of the horses a smart cut on the flank.

The steed was a spirited one and not used to the whip, and scarcely had the lash landed than he gave a wild leap into the air, came down, and broke into a mad run, dragging his mate with him. A second later the carriage struck a stone, bounced up, and Borgy was pitched out, to land in the midst of some bushes growing by the roadside.

The bolting of the team proved almost fatal to the boys in front, who scattered just in time to let horses and carriage pass them with lightning-like speed. Then the cadets gathered together and stared blankly at one another.

"It's a runaway!"

"Serves old Crabby right, for hitting the horse!"

"Yes, but he and the lady may be killed!"

Such were some of the cries. As soon as they could recover, the whole party made after the carriage, now disappearing around a bend.

"They'll never get around the next turn alive!" said Captain Harry Blossom, who was running beside Tom. Soon Dick joined the pair.

In the meantime Josiah Crabtree was filled with terror over the sudden turn of affairs. He dropped the whip and tugged first at one rein and then the other.

"Whoa! whoa!" he cried in a hoarse whisper. "Whoa!"

But instead of slackening their speed, the team moved on faster than ever, the carriage rocking violently from side to side.

"We will be killed!" moaned Mrs. Stanhope. "Oh, why did I not take Dora's advice and have a regular wedding, as she proposed!"

"I will—will stop them!" panted Crabtree. "Whoa, you brutes, whoa!"

"Whoa, Peter; whoa, Jack!" added Mrs. Stanhope timidly.

For an instant the horses seemed to take notice of the lady's voice, but only for an instant; then they went on as fast as ever, around another bend, and down a rocky stretch, lined on either side with trees and bushes.

Suddenly there came a crash, as a wheel came off the carriage. Then came a second crash and Mrs. Stanhope was hurled forth among some bushes. But the turnout continued on its way, Josiah Crabtree clinging to the wreck, until at last he too was hurled forth, to fly up among some tree branches and remain there for the best part of ten minutes.

When the crowd of cadets reached Mrs. Stanhope they found the lady unconscious and evidently suffering from a broken arm. Several of them, including Dick, Tom, and Sam, did what they could for her, while others ran off to find Josiah Crabtree and to summon a doctor.

It was several minutes before the head assistant at Putnam Hall could be helped out of the tree. He came down in fear and trembling, so overcome he could scarcely stand.

"How—how is Mrs. Stanhope?" was his, first question.

"We don't know," answered several of the cadets, and Josiah Crabtree hobbled back to find out.

The shades of night had long fallen when Mrs. Stanhope was conveyed to her home, and a doctor was brought from Cedarville and the Lanings were informed of what had happened. The doctor said that a rib as well as the left arm had been fractured, and that the lady must be kept quiet for at least two months. At once Dora set about doing what she could for her mother, and Nellie Laning remained at the homestead to assist her. No one seemed to care about Josiah Crabtree, and he was allowed to hobble back to Putnam Hall on foot.

"It was the fault of those boys," he muttered to himself. "I'll get even with them, see if I don't!"

But his chances of "getting even" while at the academy were speedily nipped in the bud by Captain Putnam, who did not say anything on Sunday, but interviewed the head assistant early on the day following.

"It is perhaps needless for us to go into the details of what has occurred, Mr. Crabtree," said the owner of the Hall. "Your contract with me comes to an end next month. I will pay you in full tomorrow and then I wish you to remove yourself and your belongings from this place."

"You—you discharge me!" cried the teacher in astonishment.

"I do. I have long been dissatisfied with your conduct toward my pupils, and I am now satisfied that you are not worthy of the position with which I entrusted you."

At this Josiah Crabtree's face fell, for he had hoped to keep his place at Putnam Hall until his marriage to Mrs. Stanhope was assured. Now there was no telling when that marriage would occur, and in the meantime it was not likely he could get another position.

"I think I ought to have more notice than this."

"You deserve no notice—since you were about to marry on the sly, so to speak, and, most likely, leave me when your contract came to an end without allowing me time to make other arrangements."

"I would have given you at least two weeks time."

"And I am giving you three weeks pay, which you do not deserve. I do not think we need to prolong the discussion," and Captain Putnam turned away.

The departure of Josiah Crabtree was hailed with satisfaction by all of the pupils excepting Dan Baxter. Strange to say, a strong friendship had sprung up between the bully and the hot-tempered school teacher. Baxter was the only one who shook hands when Crabtree left.

"I hope we meet again, Mr. Crabtree," he said. "I like you, even if the others don't."

"And I like you, Baxter," answered Josiah Crabtree. "I shall remember you."

And Josiah Crabtree did remember the bully in a manner which was strange in the extreme.

# CHAPTER XV
# DAN BAXTER'S MONEY

After the departure of Josiah Crabtree from Putnam Hall, George Strong became the leading assistant, and another teacher named Garmore took second place.

Garmore was a Yale man, and soon became as favorably known as Strong, so the pupils had nothing more to find fault with, so far as their instructors went.

As has been noted before, there were several baseball teams among the boys. As it grew too cold for baseball, these teams gave up this sport, and a good number of the lads took up football.

In this sport, Sam, being a good runner, felt very much at home, and soon he was at the head of one of the teams, playing center. Tom was also on the team, playing quarterback.

Not far from Putnam Hall was another academy kept by a certain gentleman named Pornell. The pupils at Pornell's were also great football players, and one day they sent over a challenge that the Putnams, as they were dubbed, should play them a match for the championship of the township in which both seats of learning were located.

The challenge was brought, by Peleg Snuggers, who had gone over to Pornell's on an errand for Captain Putnam.

"It's for you," said Snuggers, handing the communication to Sam. The youthful captain of the eleven broke open the letter and read it aloud:

"PORNELL ACADEMY, November 18, 189-

"To the Putnam Hall Football Team: We hereby challenge you to a game of football for the championship of the township of Cedarville, the game to be played Thanksgiving afternoon next at two o'clock, at our grounds or at your own, as you may elect. We would prefer to play on our grounds, as we have a grandstand, one-half of which will be reserved for your friends, if you will come over.

**"PORNELL FOOTBALL TEAM,**

"Per Harry Ackerson, Capt. and Secy."

"They certainly mean business," said Tom, who was in the crowd, listening to the reading of the challenge. "I go in for accepting it."

"So do I," said Larry, who played halfback.

"And I," put in Fred, who was on the right end.

The members of the football team were all at hand, and it did not take long to find out each was in favor of the game, and then the matter was laid before Captain Putnam.

"Want to play football with Mr. Pornell's lads, eh?" smiled the captain. "All right, I know of no healthier sport, rightly conducted. You shall play them, and on their grounds if you wish. But, mind you, no neglecting lessons for the sake of practicing between now and Thanksgiving!"

The pupils promised to neglect nothing, and went off with a hurrah.

Soon Peleg Snuggers was on his way to the rival academy with the following answer to the challenge:

"PUTNAM HALL, November 19, 189-

"Pornell Football Team: We hereby accept your challenge to play a game of football for the championship of the township on Thanksgiving afternoon next at two o'clock. As you have a grandstand we will play on your grounds. In return for the use of half of your stand on this occasion the senior class of our academy will put up a silver cup as a trophy, said trophy to go to the club winning the game, and to belong to that club which shall during matches to be arranged in the future win the cup three times.

**"THE PUTNAM HALL FOOTBALL TEAM,**

"Per Fred Harrison, Secy and Treas."

Dick had suggested giving the cup, and all of the senior class "chipped in" willingly, raising ten dollars, with which a very neat trophy was secured through a pupil whose father was a silversmith in New York. I say all the senior class contributed. I must correct this. There was one exception, and that was Dan Baxter.

"I haven't got anything for you or your brothers," growled the bully when Dick spoke of the matter before the class. "Let 'em furnish their own silver cups if they want 'em."

"All right, Baxter; I guess Sam and Tom will be just as well satisfied if you don't chip in," had been Dick's ready answer. "I only wanted to give everyone a chance to own an equal share in the gift, if it was desired."

"Our football team can't play for a sour apple, Dick Rover. They'll be whipped out of their boots."

"If I was a betting boy, I'd bet you a dollar on the result," answered Dick coldly.

"I'll bet you ten dollars we win!" put in Fred Garrison impulsively.

"I'll cover that bet," sneered Baxter, and drew from his pocket a roll of bills.

"Gracious, Baxter, where did you get that wad?" questioned several in chorus, for the supply of pocket money among most of the pupils was limited.

"Never mind—I have it, and that's enough," answered Baxter, but he lost no time in putting all of the money but the ten-dollar bill away.

It was all Fred Garrison could do to scrape up an equal sum, and even at that he had to borrow a dollar from Dick. But he was "game," and the money went to another pupil, who became stakeholder until the contest should be decided.

"It's a shame!" cried Sam, when he heard of the transaction. "To bet against his own school! I'm like Dick—I don't believe in betting, and yet I am glad Fred took him up. If it is in my power, Baxter shall lose his wager."

Thanksgiving was but a week off, so the football team had to work hard to get into proper condition. Moreover, studies must not be neglected, for Captain Putnam was strict, and would have canceled the game had his cadets become unmindful of their school duties. But the team got permission to get up an hour earlier than usual every morning, and this time was spent in the hardest kind of practice with the ball.

The report that Baxter had bet against his own school spread, and the bully became more unpopular than ever. But this did not daunt him, and soon he had a dozen other bets on, aggregating fifty dollars or more.

"It's a mystery to me where he gets so much money," said Dick to Captain Blossom one day, "Is his father rich?"

"I can't tell you," answered the youthful commander of Company A. "Fact of the matter is nobody knows much about Baxter—not even Mumps his chum. Nobody ever comes to see him, and he seldom ever gets any letters, yet he always has all the spending money he wants."

"Perhaps he's got a gold mine somewhere," laughed Dick.

"I don't know about that, but I do know that there are days when he hasn't a cent, and the next day he will have just such a roll of bills as you saw him with day before yesterday—and the money doesn't come to him through the mail either."

"Perhaps Captain Putnam deals it out to him."

Captain Harry shook his head. "Not much! The captain wouldn't let him have more than five dollars at a time. I've been through the mill, and I know."

Here the matter was dropped, but Dick had good cause to remember this conversation later on.

The distance from Putnam Hall to Pornell Academy was a mile and a half, and it was arranged that the football team, Captain Putnam, George Strong, and several others should ride to the latter place in the Hall carriages while the others walked the distance. Thanksgiving dawned bright and clear. The morning was spent in the Hall chapel, and dinner was served promptly at twelve.

"Don't eat too much," cautioned Sam. "I want every player to be wide awake today."

The start was signalized by a grand flourish of tin horns; and away went the two carriages with the horses on a gallop, followed by a large number of the cadets on foot, organized into their regular companies, with Major Bart Conners at the head of the battalion. The boys were in their best uniforms, and certainly presented an imposing appearance as they marched behind the music of their drums and fifes.

When the grounds at Pornell Academy were reached, they were found to be more than three quarters full, for the proprietor of the place had opened up for the benefit of the public at large, and many had come from Cedarville and the surrounding territory. The grandstand was already comfortably filled, many coming into the part reserved for the Hall folks on tickets of invitation issued by Sam and indorsed by Captain Putnam.

"Here they come!" yelled the boys of Pornell. "Three cheers for Putnam Hall!"

The cheers were given with a will; and, getting the football team and the other cadets together, Putnam Hall gave a rousing cheer in return for Pornell Academy.

Then the football teams disappeared into their respective dressing rooms, and the newly arrived cadets took their places in the grandstand. A timekeeper and referee had already been appointed by Sam and the rival captain, at a meeting at the Hall three days before.

"My! what a crowd!" exclaimed Tom, as he surveyed the multitude. "I didn't think we were going to have such an audience as this!"

"Nor I," returned Sam. "We must do our level best, fellows!"

"That's what!" came from several. "If we get whipped—"

"Remember what Baxter did—that's enough to nerve anybody on," finished Larry Colby.

"By the way, where is Baxter?"

"Sneaked out of the ranks," answered another player. "Nobody wanted to march with him."

"Well, I don't blame them," concluded Sam.

"Doctor Pornell now put in an appearance and desired to know if the football team did not wish to march around the oval escorted by his own players.

"Certainly!" cried Sam. "And to show this is a purely friendly match, let us march side by side," he went on, and this was also arranged. The Putnam Hall drum-and-fife corps led the march, and each player strode forth with a rival at his side. The march brought forth a wild round of applause and a veritable shrieking of tin horns and cracking of wooden clappers.

After the march each team was allowed quarter of an hour for practicing. The Pornellites came out first and tumbled over the leather in lively fashion. The Putnamites soon followed.

"They may be all right, but they haven't the weight," said one of the rivals. And this appeared true, for each Pornellite, man for man, was at least five pounds heavier than his opponent. But weight does not always count for everything, even in a football match.

"Time for practice is up!" came presently, and the two teams drew away from the gridiron. Then there was a toss-up for goals, and Pornell won and took the east end, that which was most favored by the slight breeze that was blowing.

And then the great game began.

# CHAPTER XVI
# THE GREAT FOOTBALL GAME

The halves were to be of twenty minutes each, so no time was lost in putting the leather into the field. It was Putnam's kick-off, and on the instant the ball went sailing into the air, to land well into Pornell's territory. Then came a grand rush, and before the words can be put down twenty-two lads were at it nip-and-tuck to get possession of the sphere.

"It's Pornell's ball!"

"Say, but ain't this going to be a snappy game!"

"Our fellows have the ball!"

"There she goes up five yards into Putnam ground!"

"Carry that ball back!" yelled Dick excitedly. "Don't let them gain an inch!"

"Whoop her up for Pornell!"

And then came a wild blare of tin horns and a waving of the academy colors, brown and white. The waving of the Hall colors, an American flag set in a border of green, came also, with an equal din from horns and wooden clappers.

"Hurrah! hurrah! hurrah!"

So, the game went on for ten minutes, and the Pornellites had gained exactly twenty-five yards—no more.

"Looks like a stand-off," said several. "Say, maybe those young soldiers aren't game!"

"That's what—but we'll wax 'em!" was the answer, and then of a sudden came another yell, for Pornell had the ball and was pushing it straight ahead for Putnam's goal.

"Ten yards!"

"Five yards more!"

"Fifteen yards more!"

"Hurrah! Hurrah! Hurrah!"

Toot! toot-a-root-toot! Clack-clack-clack, bang!

The Pornellites were now wild, but they stared blankly as they saw plucky Tom Rover snatch the leather up and run back twenty yards with it.

"He's going right through with it!"

"There goes Hardy after him!"

"Down they go!"

"Lushear has the ball! It's going back!"

"Run, Lushear, run! A dollar if you make it!"

"They can't catch him! Oh, pshaw! Down he goes!"

"But the ball is safe! A touchdown! Hurrah!"

The cry was correct. Just three minutes before the end of the first half the Pornell team scored a touchdown. Instantly preparations were made to kick a goal if possible. But the kick was a failure, and the two sides retired for the half with the score standing 4 to 0 in Pornell Academy's favor.

Glumly the Hall boys retired to their dressing room, there to be rubbed down by their chums. "It's too bad, it certainly is," came from a dozen sympathizers.

"But it can't be helped. Don't give up yet."

"They are too heavy for us in mass play," said Sam. "We must try more running away with the leather." And so it was agreed.

Soon the gong rang, and they re-entered the field.

"Now, Putnam Hall, do your best! We are looking at you!"

"They can't play a little bit," sneered Dan Baxter. "I'm ashamed of them," and he smiled to himself, thinking the fifty dollars put up on the game was already as good as won.

Sam had given his team some explicit instructions, and these were now being followed. As soon as the ball came into Putnam's possession there was a run on their part that carried the sphere twenty yards into their opponents territory.

"Go in and win, Putnam!"

"That's the way to do it!"

"Take it from them, Pornell! Go for it! Take it!"

And Pornell did take it, and half the distance gained was lost.

Both teams were now warmed up, and for fully five minutes the ball flew back and forth, remaining at the end of that time almost in the center of the gridiron.

Then Pornell tried some heavy mass play, but lost the leather on a fumble, and it came into Tom Rover's possession.

Away flew Tom, as though a legion of demons were after him, straight for Pornell's goal. The crowd began to shout itself hoarse.

"See Tom Rover! Go it, Tom, old boy, go it!"

"He can't carry it through! See, Conkey and Largren are after him!"

"There he goes down! Conkey has the leather!"

This was true, but ere Conkey could start to run Fred Garrison brought him to earth and the ball rolled out into the field.

Sam and a Pornell halfback made a rush for it.

"My ball!" yelled the Pornellite, who was twenty pounds heavier than the little captain.

"Not today!" retorted Sam, and snatched it from under his very feet. Before the Pornellite could recover from his astonishment, Sam was pelting up the field with all the nimbleness of his agile legs.

"Hurrah for Sam Rover!"

"Great Caesar! see him leg it! They can't catch him!"

"There he goes over the line!"

"A touchdown! The game is a tie!"

"Quick, fellows!" cried Sam. "Only five more minutes, remember. Who is to kick?"

It was a player named Larcom. But Larcom was not equal to it, for the wind was rising and blowing in several directions at once.

"No goal! The game is a tie!"

"Put the ball out again!"

"Only four minutes to play!"

Again the football went forth, and again the crowd pounced upon it. The Pornellites were now desperate and massed themselves as never before. They pushed forward ten yards—fifteen—twenty—almost thirty. It looked as if they would score another touchdown, if not kick a goal. But now Sam Rover sent a certain sign to his players. It was taking a risk, but it was worth trying.

The ball came over to the right of the field and spun like lightning to the left. Fred caught it up, ran ten yards, and passed it to Larry Colby, who turned it over to Tom. Away it went to Sam, and then to Frank. The Pornellites were bewildered. Where was the ball?

"Putnam has it!"

"There she goes! Hurrah for Frank Harrington. Another touchdown!"

It was true. Putnam Hall had scored another touchdown. A tremendous yelling and cheering broke out, in the midst of which the gong sounded. The game was over, and our boys had won the victory.

In a twinkle the gridiron was covered with swarming students, and Sam and his fellow players were hoisted up on willing shoulders, to be trotted around the oval. "Hurrah for Pornell!" they shouted. "Hurrah for Putnam!" came back the cry. It had been a bitter but friendly contest, and victors and vanquished shook hands over and over again.

Of course many students of Pornell were bitterly disappointed, but no one felt so sour over the whole afternoon's doing as did Dan Baxter. In all he had lost over fifty dollars, and now neither his fellow students nor the boys of Pornell Academy wanted anything to do with him. "I haven't any use for a chap who bets against his own crowd," was the comment of one academy student, and he voiced the sentiment of all. Only Mumps stuck to his chum, and the two soon left the grounds together.

By four o'clock the cadets were on their way back to Putnam Hall, the carriages moving behind the two companies of young soldiers, who sang and shouted themselves hoarse as they moved along. Even Captain Putnam entered into the spirit of the affair. "Brings me back to the days when I was a cadet myself," he said to George Strong.

Directly after supper a huge bonfire was lit on the playground, and the students were allowed to have their own fun until eleven o'clock. The football team was, of course, the center of attraction, and Sam and Tom came in for their full share of honors.

While the festivities of this Thanksgiving Eve were at their height, a sudden thought struck Dick. Captain Putnam had given the cadets permission to go beyond bounds if any cared to do so, and he hurried away, his intention being to call upon Dora Stanhope and see how she was faring. Although Dick would not admit it, he thought a great deal of Dora, and he was sorry that she was in danger of having the detestable Josiah Crabtree for a stepfather.

It was a clear, moonlight night, and he hurried off in the best of spirits, taking a short cut by way of a road through the woods. As he walked along he remembered how Tom had met in this vicinity the thief who had stolen the watch.

"I wonder if I'll meet him," he thought, but no tramp put in an appearance; indeed, he did not see a soul until the Stanhope homestead was reached.

A light was burning brightly in the sitting room, and the curtains were drawn down to within six inches of the bottom of the windows. Dick was about to ascend the porch, when he changed his mind and walked softly to one of the windows.

"If they have a lot of company I won't disturb them on a holiday like this," he thought, and peeped under one of the curtains.

The sight that met his gaze filled him with astonishment and indignation. Only two persons were present, Dora and Josiah Crabtree. Crabtree had the girl by the left wrist, and had one hand raised as if to strike his prisoner.

# CHAPTER XVII
## DICK AT THE STANHOPE COTTAGE

"The villain!"

Such were the words which sprang involuntarily to Dick's lips as he gazed at the scene before him. He was filled with bitter indignation and could hardly resist the temptation to break in the window and leap to Dora's assistance.

As he paused, he saw Dora push Crabtree back and leap to the opposite side of the center table.

"Don't you dare to touch me, Mr. Crabtree!" came loud enough for Dick to hear quite, plainly.

"I want you to behave yourself, young lady," stormed Josiah Crabtree.

"I know how to do that without your advice."

"No, you don't. You have set your mother against me. If it hadn't been for you, we would be married long ago."

"I believe a daughter has a right to advise her mother concerning a stranger, Mr. Crabtree."

"A stranger!"

"Well, an outsider—if you like that better."

"I am no outsider. I've known your mother for years. I might have married her, instead of your father doing so, if he hadn't played an underhanded trick which—"

"Stop, Sir. You shall not say a word against my father."

"Good for Dora!" thought Dick. "She's the right kind."

"Your mother is quite willing to marry me, and as a dutiful daughter you should bow to her wishes."

"Mother is not herself, Mr. Crabtree. Ever since father died she has been upset by business matters, and you have pestered the life out of her. If you would only go away for a month or so and give her time to think it over, I am sure she would end this matter between you."

"Tut, tut, child, you do not know what you are talking about! Your mother has given me her word, and you ought to bow to the inevitable."

"She has not yet married you, Sir, and until she is actually bound to you there will still be hope for her."

"This is—is outrageous!" cried Josiah Crabtree wrathfully. "Do you think I will allow a mere slip of a girl to stand between me and my plans? Just wait until I am your father—"

"You shall never take the place of my dear dead father, Mr. Crabtree—never!" and now Dora's eyes filled with tears. "He was ten thousand times better than you can ever be!"

"I must admit I can't see it. He had not half the education I possess," answered Josiah Crabtree conceitedly.

"Perhaps not, but he had an honest, warm heart, and that counts for more than a mere book education. I fancy many men are smarter, even in book learning, than Mr. Josiah Crabtree; who tried last week for an opening at Columbia College and failed to meet the requirements."

"Ha! who told you that?"

"Mother told me."

"She is foolish to take you into her confidence. It was not my fault that I failed of the opening—merely the pig-headedness of those having the matter in charge. However, I do not care much. As soon as your mother and I are married, I shall make some changes here, put up a fine brick building, and open a rival school to Putnam Hall."

"Gracious, here is news!" thought Dick. "Wonder what Captain Putnam will say to that?"

"Will you?" ejaculated Dora. "And who will give you permission to make alterations here?"

"Mrs. Crabtree—that is soon to be."

"Do you know that she holds this property in a trust for me, Mr. Crabtree? It will be hers only if I die before I become of age. Her own shares of papa's estate is situated further up the lake, at Berryport."

At this announcement Josiah Crabtree started back. "You—you are not telling the truth," he faltered.

"I am."

"But your mother is the executrix of your father's will."

"Yes."

"Exactly. Consequently she has full control of all the property until you are twenty-one."

"She has—but certain changes suggested by you or her would be subject to the approval of the court or the surrogate, so I have been told," answered Dora quietly.

Josiah Crabtree glared at the girl, and then began to pace the floor impatiently. "Dora, see here," he said finally. "Let us come to terms."

"What terms?"

"Your mother and I are bound to get married. Remove your opposition to this, and I will promise not to interfere with you in the least. You can do as you please and go where you please, and you shall have all the spending money from time to time that the estate can afford."

At this the girl's lip curled proudly. "I do not thank you for your offer, Mr. Crabtree. The whole difficulty is just here—I do not like you; and my mother shall never marry you so long as I can prevent it."

"You—you saucy minx!" he snarled and leaping around the table caught her by the wrist again. "I'll tame you before I am done with you, mark my words! If you dare to talk to your mother again—Hullo, who is this?"

"Dick Rover!" cried Dora in amazement and in delight.

For Dick had suddenly thrown up the window sash, which was unlocked, and leaped straight into the sitting room.

"Let her go, Josiah Crabtree!" ordered the young cadet. "Don't you dare to strike her, or I'll knock you flat!"

"One of the Rover boys!" muttered the ex-teacher. "What business have you here at this hour of the evening? Have you run away from the Hall?"

"Since you have been discharged, I do not feel called upon to answer your question," answered Dick. "But you must let Dora alone, or there will be a broken head around here, I can tell you that!"

At Dick's plain words Josiah Crabtree greatly paled. He had dropped the girl's wrist and now he fell back several steps.

"I was not harming the girl, only trying to reason with her."

"Oh, I know you well enough. I've heard you were the most pigheaded teacher they ever had at Putnam Hall," rejoined Dick warmly. "I shall take pains to let Mrs. Stanhope know what they think of you, too."

"Was he discharged?" asked Dora. "He told mamma that he had left of his own accord."

"He was discharged," answered Dick, who had got word through Peleg Snuggers.

"It is not true!" stormed Josiah Crabtree. "This is a—a plot to injure me in the eyes of Mrs. Stanhope, and you shall pay dearly for it, boy!" and he shook his fist in Dick's face.

"Don't do that again, Mr. Crabtree, or we may have a set-to right here— begging Dora's pardon," answered Dick, his eyes flashing fire.

"That's all right—don't give in an inch to him, Dick," whispered Dora. "I hate him—oh, more than words can tell!" and she caught the youth's arm.

"I am not afraid of you, boy!" was the short return, but now the ex-teacher turned to the hallway. "I was on the point of leaving, and now I will go, Dora. But I will be back in a day or two," and he strode from the room. A moment later he had secured his hat and overcoat and taken his departure.

"Oh, what a dreadful man!" sobbed Dora, when he was gone. "Dick Rover, what shall I do?" and she looked at him pleadingly.

"It's a puzzle to me, Dora—worse than an example in cube root in algebra!" He smiled sadly. "But if I was you I'd hold out and never let him marry my mother."

"Oh, I will never consent to that—never! But he may marry her anyway."

"If he does, you can apply to the courts for another guardian—if Crabtree doesn't treat you fairly."

"But I do not wish to separate from my mother."

"Well, the only thing to do is to keep fighting him off. In the meantime I'll try to get some folks who know Crabtree well to tell your mother just what a mean, crabbed fellow he is. Undoubtedly he is after the money your father left."

"So I always supposed—but mother does not think so."

"How is your mother?"

"She is doing nicely, and may be out in a week or two. I am keeping her in as long as possible, so that Josiah Crabtree cannot argue her into going off and getting married."

"You certainly have your hands full, Dora," answered the young cadet. "I wish I could take this burden off your shoulders, indeed I do!" and impulsively he caught up her plump, hand and kissed it.

"Oh!" She snatched the hand away and blushed prettily, but was not angry. "I—I—; it's something to know one has a friend, Dick," she said softly. "Can I come to you if I—that is if I want something done?"

"To be sure, Dora—I'll do anything in the wide world for you there!" and he kissed her hand again.

At that moment an elderly lady who had been hired to wait on Mrs. Stanhope came in, and the conversation was changed. Dora asked about life at the Hall, and Dick told of the football game and of the parts Tom and Sam had played in it.

"You are a great set of boys!" Dora smiled.

"I wish I had a couple of sisters."

"You have your two cousins, Nellie and Grace."

"Yes, but they are not as intimate as sisters would be—although they are the best of cousins."

"What does Mr. Laning say of Crabtree?" Dick whispered, as the nurse left the room for a moment.

"Uncle does not like him, but he says the whole matter is none of his affair—and mother must do as she thinks best."

It was now growing late, and Dick took his departure, kissing Dora's hand a third time as they stood in the darkness of the porch. "You're terrible!" she murmured, but it is doubtful if she meant anything by it. Girls and boys are about the same the world over and Dick's regard for Dora was of the manly sort that is creditable to anybody.

# CHAPTER XVIII
## WINTER SPORTS

"Hurrah, boys, the ice is forming just as fast as it can! We'll have skating in twenty-four hours!"

It was Sam who came rushing into the gymnasium with the news. The place was crowded at the time, for it was too cold to play on the grounds outside.

"Skating!" cried Tom. "That just suits me. I wonder if I brought my skates along?"

"You didn't," answered Sam. "Neither did I."

"I have my skates," said Fred Garrison. "Brand new pair."

"My skates were old," said Tom. "I must strike Captain Putnam for a couple of dollars of my allowance and buy a new pair."

"So must I!" put in Sam. "Dick, I know, has his skates."

It was early in December, and it had been growing colder steadily. There had been one fall of snow, but it had amounted to but little.

The next day skating in the cove of the lake near Putnam Hall was excellent, the ice being from three to four inches thick. At once Sam and Tom went to Captain Putnam.

"Want to buy some skates?" said the captain. "Well, the money I am keeping is your own, and I presume every boy likes to skate. Here are two dollars for each of you. Show me your purchases when you get back."

"We will," replied the lads, and hurried off, for time was precious, with the smooth ice waiting for them. They knew that a certain hardware dealer in Cedarville had a good quantity of skates on hand, and started to walk to the village without delay.

"Baxter is going to buy a pair of skates, too," said Sam, on the way. "I heard him telling Mumps about it."

"Well, we don't want Baxter for company," answered Tom. "He can go alone."

It did not take the lads long to reach Cedarville, but once at the hardware store considerable time was lost in getting just the skates desired.

"It's queer Baxter hasn't shown up," said Tom, when they were ready to leave.

"Perhaps he went elsewhere for his skates," suggested Sam.

The hardware shop was at the end of the village street, and as they passed a number of places of business Tom suddenly caught his brother by the arm.

"There is Baxter now—just entering that tavern!" he exclaimed in a low voice.

"The tavern!" repeated Sam. "Why, it's against the regulations to enter a drinking place!"

"I don't care—I saw Baxter go in," returned Tom. "He was with a tall man."

"If Captain Putnam hears of this, Baxter will be sent away, or at least punished."

"Perhaps, Sam; but I shan't tell him."

"No; we're no tale-bearers. Let us go up to the side windows of the tavern and see if we can see them."

This was agreed to, and the two boys hurried up to first one window and then another.

"They are not in the saloon part, that's certain," said Tom blankly. "But I saw Baxter go in, and the tall man with him."

"Here is a side room," answered Sam.

"And there they are, at a corner table. The man is giving Baxter some money!"

Tom peeped into the window over his brother's shoulder. "My gracious!"

"What's up now, Tom?"

"That tall man is the same fellow I met in the woods. The man that was with the tramp who stole the watch!"

"You don't mean it!"

"But I do! See the scar on his chin?"

"Yes."

"He is that thief's pal, as they call it."

"And he just gave Baxter some bank bills! What does it mean?"

"I give it up. But I know one thing—that man ought to be arrested!"

"That's true. Oh! they have seen us! If they—hi! what do you mean by that?"

For a burly bartender had suddenly come up behind both of the boys and hurled them backward.

"No spying around this place!" cried the dispenser of liquors roughly. "Take yourselves off!"

"There is a man inside I want to see," said Tom.

"Why don't you come in, then?"

"I will—as soon as I can find a policeman or a constable."

"What! going to have a gent arrested?"

"The man inside knows all about a stolen watch."

"You must be mistaken."

"No, I am not. Where can I find a policeman?"

"Down at the steamboat landing, most likely."

"All right. Sam, you stay here and see that that fellow don't make tracks," and Tom prepared to move away.

"See here, we don't want any trouble in our place," said the barkeeper. "We run a respectable house, we do."

"Then you ought to help me bag the pal of a thief," retorted Tom.

"Hold on, Tom!" came from Sam. "They're gone! They slipped through a back door!"

Tom ran up to the window again. It was true Baxter and the man with a scar had disappeared.

"Come on back!" he cried to his brother, and both ran to the rear of the tavern. Here there was a yard, at the end of which stood a barn and a long, low carriage shed. Only a negro hostler was in sight.

"Perhaps they haven't come out yet," began Sam, when he caught sight of a buggy on a road behind the barn. It was going at a furious rate, the scarred man driving, and lashing his mettlesome horse at the same time.

"There goes the man!"

"That's so. Where is Baxter?"

"I don't know."

They ran after the buggy, but soon gave up the chase, as man and turnout disappeared around a bend leading to the woods back of Cedarville.

"We've lost him!" murmured Tom, when he could get back his breath. "Now who in the name of Old Nick can he be?"

"Evidently a friend to Baxter. Perhaps he is Baxter's father?" suggested Sam.

"Baxter's father—Gracious! He is!"

"How do you know?"

"I'm not positive, but when I met him and the thief in the woods, the thief, who was called Buddy, started to call that fellow Baxter, but the tall man wouldn't have it, and made him call him Nolly. His right name, I feel certain, is Arnold Baxter."

"Then, if he isn't Baxter's father, he must be some close relative, otherwise he wouldn't give Baxter that money. Now it is easy to see where the bully gets all of his cash. That tall man must be rich."

"Yes, but who knows how he comes by his money? He is the chum of a thief, that's certain."

A search was made for Dan Baxter, but he could not be found. As a matter of fact, he had been in the buggy, hiding under the seat. The boys hung around for quarter of an hour longer, and then resolved to return to Putnam Hall.

"No use of making a row about it," said Tom. "I remember that policeman at the steamboat landing. He is a terribly fat fellow and evidently a hard drinker. He couldn't help us enough. We had better try to work this out on our own account. I'll tackle Baxter the first chance I get."

When the Hall was reached they looked around for the bully, but found he had not returned. They had now to go in for their studies, and for the time being the affair was dropped.

That afternoon found them on the lake, and while enjoying the skating Dick was informed of what had occurred. "A bad crowd," said the elder Rover. "Yes, tackle Baxter, by all means. But be cautious what you say, for you can't prove much, remember."

A race had been arranged between the boys, and Dick was one of the contestants. The distance was from one end of the cove to the other was a little over three-quarters of a mile. There were ten starters, including Fred,

Frank, Larry, and Mumps. Mumps had a reputation as a skater, gained at his home on the Hudson River.

"All ready?" shouted the starter.

There was a dead silence.

"Go!" came the word, and away went the ten, their skates flashing brightly in the setting sun. Soon Larry Colby was in advance, with Mumps just over his shoulder.

"It is Larry's race!"

"Mumps is a close second!"

"Shake 'em up, Fred! What are you lagging about, Frank? Go it, Leo!"

Skirk skirk skirk went the skate runners, and now a crowd of lads started in pursuit of the racers. Soon the turning point was gained. Larry was in advance still, but now Mumps overtook him, and suddenly the boy from the Hudson who had such a reputation as a racer shot fifteen feet in advance. It looked as if the race was certainly his, and Larry and the others felt much downcast.

# CHAPTER XIX
# THE SKATING RACE—DAN
# BAXTER IS CORNERED

The wind had been with the racers thus far, but as one after another of the skaters turned the mark they found the wind now full in their faces, and it was blowing freshly.

"Mumps will win beyond a doubt!" was the cry, as the lad from the Hudson River forged still further ahead.

"My skate is loose!" cried Larry, and a second later the skate came off and flew fifty feet away.

By this time Dick and Fred were coming up, slowly but surely. It seemed to be nip-and-tuck between them, and the friends of each cheered wildly.

"Go it, Dick; you can come in second anyway!"

"Make him follow you, Fred! You can do it if you try!"

On and on went the racers, Mumps still ten feet ahead, Fred and Dick side by side, and the others in a bunch just back of them.

But the strain was now beginning to tell upon Mumps, who had pushed himself too much from the start. Halfway to the finish from the turning point Dick and Fred began to crawl up, until they were less than a yard behind him, one at either hand.

"Go it, Mumps! They are catching you!"

Mumps did try to increase his speed, but his wind was gone and he could hardly strike out. The finish was now in sight, and the boys began to shout on every side:

"Go it, every one of you!"

"Hurrah! Mumps, Dick, and Fred are a tie!"

It was true the three boys were side by side. But presently both Dick and Fred made extra efforts and forged ahead.

"It's your race, Fred!"

"It's yours, Dick!"

But it was neither's race—for with a shout both whizzed over the line at the same instant.

"A tie!"

"And Mumps ain't in it!"

"Three cheers for Dick and Fred!" shouted Frank Harrington, and the cheers were given with a will. By this time the play hour was over, and all of the skaters rushed back to the Hall, to get ready for the drill previous to supper. It is needless to add that each lad brought an extra big appetite with him.

All of the Royer boys noticed that Dan Baxter did not turn up at roll call, nor did the bully put in an appearance that night. "Got a day off," said Mumps, but that was all he could tell.

Late on the following day Tom was walking toward the gymnasium when he caught sight of Baxter just entering the school grounds. He at once ran toward the bully.

"Baxter, I want to have a talk with you," he said sharply, as he looked the bully squarely in the face.

"Do you?" was the uneasy answer. "All right, fire ahead."

"Hadn't you better come up to the dormitory? We can have it all to ourselves, for the others are either in the gymnasium or on the lake."

"Well, I was going up to our dormitory anyway," answered Baxter, and stalked off, leaving Tom to follow him. Once they were in the dormitory occupied by the bully and his set, Baxter locked the door.

"Now out with what you have got to say, and be quick about it," he growled.

"I want to know who that man was, you met in the tavern in Cedarville."

"Didn't meet any man in particular. Met half a dozen in general."

"You know the man I mean—the tall fellow, with a scar on his chin."

"Oh, that fellow? I think his name is Nolly. He's a book agent, and I promised to buy some histories from him," and Baxter pretended to yawn, as if he was not especially interested.

"You are not telling the truth, Baxter," answered Tom, undaunted by this show of nerve.

"Do you mean to say I lie, Rover? Take care, or you may be sorry for what you say!"

"You can't pull the wool over my eyes, Baxter. That man's name is no more Nolly than mine is George Washington or yours William McKinley."

"Isn't it? Then perhaps you know his real name."

"I do. His name is Arnold Baxter."

Had a bomb exploded at Baxter's ear he would not have appeared more astonished.

"Say, who told you that?" he demanded fiercely and caught Tom by the arm.

"Let go of me, Dan Baxter."

"I say, who told you that?"

"I heard his name in the woods. He was with the man who robbed my brother Dick of his watch, when we were at home."

"Stuff and nonsense!" growled the bully, but he was very pale, and his voice shook with emotion. "That man's name is William Nolly. He used to know my father. That is why I helped him along by giving him an order for the histories. I don't really want the books."

"If you was helping him, how is it that Sam and I saw you taking a roll of bills from him down at the tavern?"

Again Baxter started. "You didn't see no such thing!" he roared, regardless of his grammar. "I—that is—he gave me some change, that is all. Here are the books I bought," and he pointed to a package he had been carrying.

"It's a made-up story," retorted Tom. "He gave you money, and my opinion is that that man is your father, and that he is no better than the man with whom he associates."

The words had scarcely left Tom's lips than Baxter leaped upon him—like an enraged animal and hurled him to the floor. "I've a good mind to—to kill you for that, Rover!" he hissed. "Take it back, or I'll choke you to death!" and his strong hand sought Tom's throat.

"Will you!" came in a gasp, and now Tom turned over and threw the bully to one side. "I guess two can play at this game. Take that!" and he struck Baxter a heavy blow on the side of the face. In a moment they had clinched and were trying their best to throw each other.

Suddenly came a rattle of the door knob. "Boys! Boys! What does this mean?" It was George Strong's voice. "Open the door instantly."

"Keep your mouth shut!" whispered Baxter, as he again shook his fist in Tom's face. "Not one word—on your life!"

Then he disengaged himself, adjusted his collar and tie, which had become rumpled, and unlocked the door. At once the head assistant strode into the dormitory.

"Have you two been fighting?" he demanded.

"We were only boxing a bit, sir," answered Baxter, before Tom could speak. "No harm intended, sir."

"You were making a good deal of noise," answered George Strong dryly. "What have you to say, Rover?"

"I have this to say, Mr. Strong," answered Tom boldly. "I would like to interview Captain Putnam without delay."

"Don't you dare—" began Baxter, when a wave of the teacher's hand cut him, short.

"About what, Rover?"

"About this affair, and about Baxter, sir. I am not a telltale, but certain things have happened which I think Captain Putnam should know for his own sake and for the reputation of his school."

"You—you imp!" hissed Baxter. He wanted to spring at Tom, but now George Strong caught him and held him fast.

"Baxter, you had best come with me—and you too, Rover."

"To see Captain Putnam?" queried Tom.

"Yes."

"I don't want to go," blustered the bully. "Let Rover tell his yarn—I don't care. It will be only another of his lies."

"Then you shall go to the guardroom," said the teacher. "Rover, you may go to see the captain alone."

"I will sir—at once," and Tom made away. He had no sooner departed than George Strong marched Baxter off to the guardroom previously described. As the pair passed down the stairs they encountered Mumps coming up.

"Hullo, Dan, what does this mean?" asked Mumps in wonder.

"I'm under arrest," laughed Baxter bitterly. "And for nothing, too."

"Silence!" commanded George Strong. "If you have done nothing wrong, you will soon be released."

"You bet I will," rejoined Baxter insolently, and then, watching his chance, he made a sign which Mumps well understood. The sign meant "Come and help me if you can."

Mumps nodded to show that he understood. Then he pretended to go up to the dormitory, while the head teacher conducted Baxter to the guardroom, locked the impudent one in, and walked away with the key.

# CHAPTER XX
## THE BULLY LEAVES PUTNAM HALL

"So you wish to see me, Rover? Very well, come right in and sit down," said Captain Putnam, who sat in front of his desk, making up some of his accounts for the month just past.

Tom came in and sat down. It must be confessed he was a trifle nervous, but this soon wore away.

"I came to tell you something and to ask your advice," he began. "You remember what happened to me when I ran away into the woods just after arriving at the Hall?"

"Very well, Thomas," and the captain smiled.

"Well, when Sam and I went to Cedarville to buy our skates we saw Dan Baxter in the tavern there, in company with the man with a scar on his chin. This man gave Baxter some bank bills."

"What! At the tavern?"

"Yes, Sir."

"Please tell your story in detail, Rover," and now Captain Putnam swung around so that he might get a full view of his pupil's face.

And Tom told his story from beginning to end just as I have set it down in the foregoing pages.

"I am certain this man is some relative of Baxter," he concluded. "And I am equally certain he is not an honest fellow."

"Humph!" Captain Putnam arose and began to pace the heavily carpeted floor. "Rover, this is a serious charge."

"I understand that, Sir. But you can't blame us boys for trying to get back Dick's watch and trying to—to—"

"Bring the guilty party to justice? Certainly not! But it would seem the man with a scar is not the thief."

"No, but he is the boon companion of the thief."

"That is true—unless there is some grave mistake. But you are right about one thing, the man is really Baxter's father, and his name is Arnold Baxter."

"And why does he travel around under the name of Nolly?"

"That is the mystery. I met Mr. Baxter only once—when he placed his son in my care. At that time I was certain he was wearing a wig and a false mustache. The scar was on his chin, although he tried to hide it. I have never seen him since. When any money is due from him he sends it to me by mail and does not ask for any receipt. I once asked Baxter about his parents, and he said his mother was dead and he didn't know exactly where his father was, as the latter was a great traveler and went everywhere."

"I see."

"If you are right, and the man is a rascal, it is to his credit that he is trying to bring his son up as a gentleman. Perhaps he doesn't want Daniel to know anything of the past. Do you follow me?"

"I do, sir. But if this is so, would he take his son into the tavern?"

"Perhaps—everybody is not so opposed to drinking as I am."

"Well, if Mr. Baxter is a bad man, I rather think Dan is a chip of the old block," rejoined Tom bluntly. "But be that as it may, all I want to get hold of is that thief and Dick's timepiece."

"I will question Baxter closely," answered Captain Putnam. "But I do not wish to hold him guilty of something of which most likely he knows nothing."

George Strong had by this time come in, and he was sent to bring Baxter. He was gone but a few minutes when he came back in high excitement.

"Baxter has broken out of the guardroom!" he, exclaimed. "I cannot find him anywhere!"

"Did you look in the dormitory?"

"Yes, sir; and his valise is gone, and his trunk is empty of all of value."

"Humph!" Captain Putnam's brow contracted. "This looks very suspicious."

At that moment one of the smaller cadets came in with a note in his hand.

"I just met Baxter running down the road!" exclaimed the little fellow. "He gave me this for you, Captain Putnam."

At once the proprietor of the Hall tore open the communication and read it half aloud:

"Good-by to Putnam Hall forever. It is full of fellows who are no good and run by a man I never liked. No use of following me, for I am going to join my father, and I don't mean to come back.

**"DAN BAXTER**

"P. S.—Tell the Rover boys I shan't forget them, and some day I shall take pains to square accounts.

**"D. B."**

"The foolish boy," was the captain's comment. "But perhaps he has done what is best, for it might have been necessary to dismiss him." For a long while those at the Hall wondered how Baxter had escaped. Only Mumps knew and he kept the secret to himself. A duplicate key to the door of the guardroom had done the trick.

As Baxter was not followed, nothing more was spoken of him for the time being, and after several days the cadets settled down to their regular work as though nothing out of the ordinary had occurred. A hunt was instituted by Dick for Arnold Baxter and Buddy the thief, but no trace of the pair came to light.

The Christmas holidays were now at hand and the closing days at Putnam Hall were given over to several entertainments. One of these consisted of a stage performance of a play called "A Christmas in a Tenement," given by twelve of the boys. Three of the lads, including Tom, took female parts, and the audience laughed itself sore over the antics that were cut up.

Many living in the vicinity came to the entertainment; including all of the Lanings and also Dora Stanhope and her mother; who was now almost as well as ever.

"It was fine!" said Nellie Laning to Tom. "But, oh, Tom, what a girl you did make!"

"Wouldn't you like me for a sister?" queried Tom.

"A sister! Oh, dear!" cried Nellie, and began to laugh again.

"You looked like a female giraffe!" put in Grace Laning. "Sam acted a little boy splendidly. Sam, don't you want a stick of candy?"

"Yes, mammy, please," squeaked Sam, just as he had on the stage, and another laugh went around.

In the meantime Dick had drawn Dora to one side. "What is the news?" he asked anxiously.

"Nothing new," sighed Dora. "Josiah Crabtree has gone to Boston on business. I am afraid I cannot keep that marriage off much longer. He seems bound to marry mother, and even if she feels like drawing back she hasn't the courage to tell him so."

"It's a shame," murmured Dick. "Well, remember what I said, Dora, if I can ever help you I will." And he squeezed her hand. Before they separated he gave her a silk handkerchief he had purchased at Cedarville, one with her initial in the corner, and she blushingly handed over a scarf made by herself. Dick was very proud of that scarf, although Tom and Sam teased him about it unmercifully.

Of course the boys had received letters from their uncle and aunt regularly, yet they watched eagerly for the hour that should bring them within sight of the farm with its well-known buildings. The journey to Oak Run proved uneventful, and here Jack, the hired man, met them with the carriage.

"Glad to see you, lads," he said—with a grin.

"Seems quite natural like."

"So it does, Jack!" cried Tom. "Let 'em out, for we want to get home!"

The snow was falling, and by the time the farmhouse was reached it was several inches deep. "We're in for a sleigh ride before we go back," said Sam.

Their uncle and aunt stood at the door to receive them. "Welcome home! Merry Christmas!" came from both, and each of the boys gave a warm handshake to Randolph Rover and hearty kiss to their Aunt Martha. Past troubles were all forgotten.

This was Christmas Eve, and the boys stayed up late, cracking nuts by the blazing log fire and having a good time generally.

In the morning Dick was the first one awake.

"For gracious' sake!" he ejaculated, staring at the chimney piece. "There hung his own stocking and also one each belonging to Tom and Sam. Each was filled with goodies such as he knew only his Aunt Martha could make.

"Sam and Dick, wake up, we've struck a bonanza!" he cried, and hauled both from under the covers. All laughed heartily, and marched down to the dining room with the stockings over their shoulders.

"A merry Christmas to Uncle Randolph from all of us," said Tom, handing over a much coveted volume on agriculture. "And a merry Christmas to Aunt Martha from three bad boys," added Sam, and turned over a fancy work-basket, both presents having been purchased at Ithaca on the journey home.

"Ha! Just what I desired!" said Randolph Rover, adjusting his spectacles. "I am very much obliged, boys—I am, indeed!"

"Such a pretty basket!" murmured Mrs. Rover. "It was very good of you!" and she, hugged each lad in his turn. Then came more presents—neckties, collars, and gloves for the boys, besides a book for each written by a favorite juvenile writer.

"The snow is two feet deep!" said Dick, after an inspection, when breakfast had come to an end. "We're booked for the house today!"

"We'll wait until afternoon," said Mr. Rover.

It was a happy time, even if they were snowed in. Soon the warm sun came out and brought the snow down a little. "Best kind of sleighing now," said the hired man, and drove around the biggest sleigh on the place. All tumbled in, and the party did not return until after midnight.

# CHAPTER XXI
## SOMETHING ABOUT THE PAST

During holiday week the boys took occasion to tell their uncle all of the particulars concerning the tramp called Buddy, Arnold Baxter, and his son the bully. It is needless to state that Randolph Rover listened to their story with interest.

"I would like to meet this man with a scar on his chin," he said. "Speaking of him reminds me of something that happened years ago."

"What was it, Uncle Randolph?" questioned Tom.

"Your father had an enemy who had a scar on his chin."

"What!" cried Sam. "Could it have been this Arnold Baxter?"

"Hardly, although such a thing is possible. This man was a Westerner, and laid claim to some property owned by your father. They had a quarrel, and the fellow shot your father in the arm and then ran away. I never learned any of the particulars."

"Arnold Baxter and this Buddy spoke about a mining claim, and about some papers," burst out Tom. "I'd like to wager he is the same chap!"

"If he is, you want to beware of him," responded Randolph Rover gravely. "He is your father's deadliest enemy."

"I'll remember that," said Dick, and his brothers nodded. The matter was talked over for several hours, but brought little satisfaction.

On New Year's Day came another fall of snow, and the lads spent the afternoon in a regular snowballing match among themselves and with the hired man. Poor Jack caught it on all sides, and after quarter of an hour's bombardment was glad enough to run to the barn, for shelter. "But it's great sport," he grinned, as he almost stood on his head trying to get from the back of his neck a soft snowball which Tom had planted there.

The following day they started back for Putnam Hall, and on the way met Larry, Frank, Fred, and a number of others. When Ithaca was reached a surprise awaited the crowd. The weather was so cold that the ice impeded transportation, and the Golden Star was not making her usual trips to Cedarville and other points.

"Here's a state of things!" cried, Tom. "What's to do—walk to Putnam Hall?"

"Well, hardly, seeing that it is a good number of miles and the weather is bitterly cold."

"Well, if we can't walk and can't ride, how are we to get there?" came from Sam.

"That's the conundrum, Brudder Bones," laughed Larry, imitating a negro minstrel. "I'se gib it up, sah!"

"It's no laughing matter," said Dick. "We might stay in Ithaca over night, but traveling may be no better in the morning."

"Let us send a telegram to Captain Putnam for instructions," suggested Fred, and soon the following message was prepared and sent to the Hall by way of Cedarville:

"Six of us are held up at Ithaca by the cold. How shall we come on?"

This message was forwarded without delay, and while awaiting an answer Dick and his brothers took a walk through the town.

They were passing down the main street when Sam uttered a short cry.

"Hullo, there is Josiah Crabtree!"

"Where?" questioned Dick with deep interest.

"Across the way. He has just entered the jewelry store on the corner."

"Say, perhaps he's buying a wedding ring," blurted out Tom before he stopped to think.

"Tom, that matter is no joke," came from Dick, as his face grew red. "I sincerely hope, for Dora Stanhope's sake, that he never marries, Dora's mother."

"Oh, so do I," answered Tom readily.

"Why, he isn't fit to be stepfather to a dog!"

"Let us look into the window and see what he is doing," suggested Dick uneasily, for he could not get it out of his head but that his brother's guess might be correct.

The window was broad and clear, and they looked through it into the shop with ease. Josiah Crabtree stood at the counter, talking to a clerk, who presently brought forth a tray of plain rings.

"It is a wedding ring, as sure as you are born!" cried Tom.

"I'm going in," said Dick in a low tone. "Wait for me here," and he entered the establishment. There were counters on both sides, and he walked to a position directly opposite to that occupied by the ex-schoolmaster.

"I wish to see some cheap scarf pins," he said to the clerk who came to wait on him, and the man hurried off to bring on the articles mentioned.

"And is this the latest style of wedding ring?" Dick heard Josiah Crabtree say in a low voice.

"Yes, sir, the very latest—and very tasty," answered the clerk who was waiting on him.

"I wish two, one for the lady and one for—ahem—myself."

"Yes, sir—quite the style now for a gentleman to have a ring. Want them engraved, of course."

"Yes. Here is a paper with the sizes and what is to be engraved upon each. How much will they be with the engraving?"

"Six dollars each, sir."

"Six dollars! Don't you make a reduction on taking two?" asked Crabtree, who was a good deal of a miser.

"We can throw off a dollar on the pair," answered the clerk, after consulting the proprietor of the shop.

"I didn't expect to pay over ten dollars."

"We can give you this style for ten dollars."

"No, I want the latest—to please the lady."

"Humph!" muttered Dick. "You'll never please Mrs. Stanhope with any ring."

"Eleven dollars is the lowest we can take."

"And when will the rings be ready for me?"

"Day after tomorrow. We might do them quicker, but we have a great deal of engraving ahead."

"Day after tomorrow will do, for I do not wish them until next week," answered Josiah. "Here is my card. I am stopping at the American House in this city."

"Yes, sir. Do you want the rings sent?"

"No, I will call for them," concluded the ex-teacher, and hurried from the place. Sam and Tom saw him coming, and dodged out of sight around the corner.

Dick had taken in all that was said and had in the meantime picked out a cheap scarf pin which cost but ten cents. As soon as Crabtree was gone he paid for the pin, shoved it into his pocket, and rejoined his brothers, to whom he told the particulars of what had occurred.

"He intends to marry Mrs. Stanhope next week," he declared bitterly. "I would give almost all I'm worth to stop that wedding."

"Gracious, but you do think a heap of Dora!" said Tom slyly.
"Well, I don't blame you. She is a splendid girl—eh, Sam?"

"That's right," answered Sam.

"But, Dick, why not put up a job on old Crabtree?"

"What kind of a job?"

"Find out just when he wants to get married and then send him a letter from Yale or some other college, requesting him to come on at once if he wants a certain position. That will cause another delay, and maybe Mrs. Stanhope will get sick of him."

"Oh, if only we could do something like that!" cried his elder brother quickly. "I wish I could send him away out West."

"We'll manage it somehow—" put in Tom.

"Sam, what wonderful ideas you have for your years!"

"Oh; I take after my big brothers," answered the youngest Rover modestly.

Late in the evening a telegram was received from Captain Putnam:

"Remain in Ithaca over night, at the American House. Will send word how to get here in the morning."

"The American House!" ejaculated Dick. "That is where old Crabtree is stopping."

"If only we can have some fun with the old chap!" sighed Tom.

The six boys marched to the hotel in a body, told their story, and showed the telegram to the clerk.

"All right," said the clerk. "We've had cadets stop here before. I have a big room on the second floor, with two large beds in it. Will that do?"

"That suits me," said Larry.

"Is Mr. Josiah Crabtree stopping here?" questioned Tom.

"Yes. He has the room next to the one I mentioned—his is No. 13, and yours will be No. 14."

"All right; thanks," answered Tom dryly, and immediately began to lay plans for playing a joke on the old teacher.

"We don't want to let Mr. Crabtree know we are stopping here," he said to the clerk later on. "He is no longer a teacher at the Hall, and we would rather not meet."

"Shall I put you in another room?"

"Oh, no; only don't tell him we are here."

"I'll remember that, sir."

As soon as the boys had been shown to the big room, Tom turned to his fellows. "I want each of you to chip in ten cents," he said.

"What for?" came in a chorus.

"For the purpose of getting square with old Crabby."

"I don't see the connection," said Larry. "Kindly be a little more definite."

"You'll see, or hear, the connection a little later on," answered Tom. "Quick, shell out and I'll promise you your money's worth, or return the amount with legal interest."

The fifty cents was quickly collected, and, adding ten cents of his own, Tom ran from the hotel. "No fish market open at this time of night," he said to himself.

"I'll have to try a restaurant," and hurried into the first place which came into sight.

"Have you any crabs?" he asked, of the waiter who came to him.

"Yes, sah; very fine, sah. Want some soft-shell, sah?"

"I don't care whether they are soft-shell or as hard as rocks. I want live crabs, the most active kind you have in stock."

The waiter stared in amazement, then called the owner of the restaurant.

"You want live crabs?"

"I do—strong, active, go-ahead crabs, and I want them in a box."

"Is this a joke?"

"It will be—when the crabs get to work," answered Tom with a wink.

"Oh, I understand," laughed the restaurant keeper. "How many?"

"What are they worth?"

"Good nippers are worth ten cents apiece."

"Give me six, and mind you put them in a strong box for me."

Five minutes later Tom left the restaurant with the live crabs tucked safely away in a shoe box under his overcoat.

# CHAPTER XXII
## FUN AT THE HOTEL

It was no easy matter for Tom to get into the room Josiah Crabtree was occupying, but after trying a good number of keys, fished up here, there, and everywhere, one was at last found that fitted the lock.

Striking a match, Tom entered the room quickly, drew back the sheet of the bed, dumped in the crabs, and then pulled the sheet up to its original place.

"He's coming!" whispered Sam, who stood guard at the door. "Hide, Tom," and then he ran back to the big room adjoining.

Finding he could not escape, Tom threw the box under the bed and rushed to a closet in the corner. Here he crouched down behind a large trunk left in the place on storage. He had scarcely secreted himself when Josiah Crabtree came in. He had shoved his key in the lock, but had failed to notice that the lock-bolt was already turned back.

"Oh, what a cold night," muttered the ex-school teacher as he lit the gas. "A warm bed will feel fine."

"I reckon it will be warm enough," thought Tom.

As the room was scantily heated, Crabtree lost no time in disrobing. Having donned a long night robe, he turned off the gas, flung the sheets back, and leaped into bed.

Exactly ten seconds of silence followed. Then came a yell calculated to raise the dead.

"Whow! What's this? Oh! What's got me by the legs? Oh, oh! oh! I'm being eaten up alive! Let go there! Oh, dear!"

And with additional yells, Josiah Crabtree leaped straight out of bed, one crab hanging to his left knee, several on his feet, and one, which he had caught hold of clinging to the back of his hand. At once he began to do an

Indian war-dance around the apartment, knocking the furniture right and left.

"Let go there! What on earth can they be? Oh, my toe is half off—I know it is! Let go!" And then he struggled toward the gas jet, but before he could light it Tom had slipped out of the apartment, closing the door behind him. The banging of furniture continued, and then came a crash, as the washstand went over, carrying with it a bowl, a soap tray, and a large, pitcher filled with water. The icy water gushed over Crabtree's feet, making him shiver with the cold, but the crabs were undaunted and only clung the closer.

The noise soon aroused the entire hotel, and the clerk, several bell-boys, and finally the proprietor, rushed to the scene. The door was flung wide open.

"Have you been drinking, sir? How dare you disturb the hotel in this fashion?" demanded the proprietor.

"The crabs! Take them off!" yelled Crabtree, continuing to dance around.

"Crabs? What made you bring crabs up here?"

"I—I—oh, my toes! Take them off!" shrieked Josiah Crabtree, and kicked out right and left. One of the crabs was flung off, to land in the hotel proprietor's face and to catch the man by the nose.

"My nose! He will bite it off!" cried the hotel man. "Kill the thing, Gillett—smash it with a-a-anything!"

And Gillett, the clerk, tried to do so, while the hotel man and Crabtree continued to dance around in the wildest kind of fury. Safe in their own room, the boys laughed until they cried. All had gone to bed, and Tom lost no time in getting under the covers.

"Somebody has played a trick," began Crabtree when an extra nip on his knee cut him short. "Oh, my, I shall die!" he moaned. "I know I shall die!"

By this time the proprietor of the hotel had freed himself from the crab that had nipped him on the nose. "You won't die, but you'll get out of this hotel," he snarled. "Throw the crabs out of the window," he continued to his employees, and after a good deal of trouble one crab after another was hurled forth, the window being kept open in the meantime and the icy draught causing Crabtree to shiver as with the ague. As there seemed no help for it the ex-teacher began to dress again with all possible speed.

"If I find out who did this I'll—I'll kill him," moaned Josiah Crabtree. "I've been nipped is a hundred places!"

"You'll leave this hotel!" said the proprietor. "I've had enough of you. First the room didn't suit, then the price was too high, and at dinner and supper you found all manner of fault with the menu. You'll go, and the quicker, the better."

"But look here—" began Crabtree.

"I won't argue with you. Either get out or I'll have you arrested as a disorderly character."

"Yes, but—"

"Not a word. Will you go quietly, or shall I have you put out?"

"I'll—I'll go!" gasped Josiah Crabtree, and five minutes later he was on the cold street, satchel in hand, and saying all manner of unpleasant things under his breath.

"Oh, Tom!" laughed Sam, and could go no further. Each of the boys had felt like exploding a dozen times. It was not until an hour after that any of them managed to get to sleep.

When they came down in the morning the hotel clerk winked at them. "I'm not saying a word," he whispered. "But it served the old crank right. Even the boss is doing a little smiling, although he got quite a nip himself."

"Really, I don't know what you are talking about," answered Tom. Then he shut up one eye, stuck his tongue into his cheek, and strolled into the dining room.

"He's an out-and-out boy, he is," murmured the clerk, gazing after him.

Breakfast was finished, and the cadets were strolling around the hotel awaiting further instructions from Captain Putnam, when a man drove up to the door in a big livery-stable sleigh.

"I am after some boys bound for Putnam Hall," he said. "Captain Putnam telegraphed to the boss to bring 'em up to the Hall in this sleigh."

"Hurrah!" shouted Sam. "Such a long ride will just suit me!"

"If it doesn't prove too cold," was Dick's comment.

There was but one seat in the turnout, the back being filled with straw and robes. "Take your lunch with you," said the driver. "For it's a long trip we have before us, and I reckon a part of the road ain't none too good."

The clerk of the hotel was consulted, and soon a big lunch-box was packed, containing sandwiches, cake, and a stone jug of hot coffee. This was stowed away in the straw, and the lads piled in, laughing merrily over the prospect before them.

"Off we go!" shouted Larry, and with a crack of the whip the sleigh started. It was drawn by a heavy pair of horses, who looked well able to get through any snowdrift that might present itself.

Ithaca was soon left behind, and they sped swiftly along a road running northward, a half mile more from the west shore of the lake. The road was level, and somewhat worn by travel, and for the first three miles good time was made.

"If we can continue this gait we'll reach Putnam Hall by three or four o'clock this afternoon, allowing an hour's rest at noon," said the driver in reply to a question put by Frank. "But we have still a number of small hills to climb, and it's not going to stay as clear as it was early this morning."

The latter remark was caused by the sun disappearing under heavy clouds. Soon it began to snow, at first lightly, and then heavier and heavier.

"We're going to catch it!" said Tom, after the noon stop had been taken at a wayside hotel, where they had taken dinner, keeping the boxed lunch for later on. "The snow is four inches deeper than it was."

On they went again, the snow becoming so thick at last that they could scarcely see a yard before them. It was very cold, and the cadets were glad enough to huddle in the straw, with the robes over them, leaving the driver to pick his way as best he could.

An hour had gone by, and they were wondering if they were anywhere near Cedarville, when a wild shout rang out, and the next instant came a crash, as their sleigh collided with another coming from the opposite direction. A runner of each turnout was smashed, and the occupants of the other sleigh came tumbling in upon the lads in great confusion.

"Great Caesar! what's this?" groaned Tom as he shifted a weight from his shoulders, and then he stared in amazement as he found himself confronted by Nellie Laning!

"Tom Rover!" burst from the girl's lips soon as she could recover her breath. "Did you ever!"

"Well, hardly!" murmured Tom, as he helped her to, a sitting position. "You're coming in on us fast. What's the trouble? Oh, and there is Grace and your father!"

"The sleighs ran into each other," answered Nellie. "Can you stop the horses, father?" she called out.

"Yes, but the sleigh is a goner," answered Mr. Laning, and then some sharp words passed between himself and the livery-stable driver. There was no doubt, however, but that the blinding storm was largely responsible for the accident.

An examination proved that both sleighs would have to be abandoned, and then the two parties sought shelter at a near-by farmhouse, while Mr. Laning went off on one horse, and the livery-stable driver on another, each to borrow a sleigh elsewhere.

This left the boys in the company of the girls for over an hour, and during that time Dick, Tom and Sam asked a great many questions, especially about Mrs. Stanhope and Dora.

"Yes, the marriage is to come off next week, Thursday, unless something prevents it," said Nellie. "Dora is fairly sick over the prospect. What Aunt Lucy can see in Mr. Crabtree is more than any of us can understand."

"He must have hypnotized her," observed, Dick. "It's a shame! I wish old Crabtree was in Jericho!"

"So do all of us!" laughed Grace, and then Sam took her off for a quiet chat, while Tom, monopolized Nellie.

"Those Rover boys think a great deal of the Lanings and Stanhopes," observed Larry to Fred. "Well, it's all right—they are awfully nice girls, every one of 'em!"

# CHAPTER XXIII
# BALLOTING FOR A SECOND LIEUTENANT

"Back to Putnam Hall at last! How home-like the place looks!" Sam uttered the words as he leaped from the sleigh and ran for the main entrance, where Captain Putnam stood to receive them. He had heard of the accident, and was fearful that one or another of his pupils might have been hurt.

"Thank Providence that no one was killed or seriously injured!" he observed, as he wrung each by the hand. "Welcome, lads, and I trust you have all had happy holidays."

"The same to you, Captain Putnam!" cried one after another, and then they passed in to be greeted by George Strong and the new assistant.

Cadets kept coming back for three days, on the following Monday the regular school opened, to end in July. Soon the boys were as deep in their studies as ever before.

In the meantime Dick had concocted a scheme for sending Josiah Crabtree on a goose chase to Chicago. Tom had a friend in that city, and he was requested to mail without delay a certain letter which Tom enclosed with his own.

This letter was composed by Dick. It was written on a large letter-head upon which Dick printed the advertisement of the "Mid-West National College, Incorporated," doing the work on a small printing press used by some of the boys in getting out a school monthly. To make the letter even more imposing, Dick printed the body of it on a typewriter which was used by one of the classes taking a business course. The letter ran as follows:

"JOSIAH CRABTREE, A. M., Cedarville, N., Y.

"CHICAOO, January 1, 189-.

"Dear Sir: You have been recommended to us by a New York scholastic employment agency as a first-class teacher in mathematics, history, and other branches. We are in immediate need at the opening of this term of such a teacher, and will pay two thousand dollars per year. Will you come on at once, at our expense, with a view to closing with us? Our institution is a new one, but we already have eighty pupils, of the best families of the Middle West, and are certain to have fifty more before the end of the year. We understand that you are a bachelor, which state just suits our wants. Kindly wire us and come on before Thursday the 10th, if possible. The two thousand per year is, of course, exclusive of board and suite of rooms, which, we provide for all of our instructors.

"Yours truly,

"ANDREW N. BLUFF, LL.D., President."

"If that doesn't make old Crabtree hustle then I miss my guess," said Tom after reading the communication. "He loves money too well to let that two thousand slide—marriage or no marriage. Even if he wants to wed, he'll go West to try and fix it up to hold the position anyway."

The letter was posted to the friend in Chicago that very night. On the letter to Josiah Crabtree was placed an address in Cedarville which was certain to catch him.

On the following day Captain Putnam, announced an election for second lieutenant of Company A. "Lieutenant Darman will not be here any longer, as his family have moved to England," he said. "I trust you elect the best cadet possible to the office. The election takes place next Wednesday at noon."

At once a lively discussion took place. There were half a dozen pupils who wanted the position, and among them were Dick, Fred, and Mumps.

"I ought to have that place," said Mumps, and on the quiet he started to buy up votes where he could not influence them in any other way. This move succeeded among the smaller lads, but the big boys turned from him with scorn.

It must be confessed that Dick was exceedingly anxious when the time for balloting arrived. Would he succeed or fail?

Just before dinner Captain Putnam brought out a square box into which ballots might be cast.

"The cadets will stand up in a row to be counted," he said. "Major Conners, will you will kindly count your command."

"Eighty-seven, including myself," announced the youthful major, after he had gone down the line and back with care.

"Are any cadets absent?"

"No, sir."

"Very well then, we will proceed to vote by having each cadet come up and cast a slip of paper with his favorite's name on it in the box. The line will march in single file, one pace from man to man. Forward!"

The captain stood by the ballot box, and up came the file, Major Conners first and Captain Blossom following. In a few minutes all of the eighty-seven ballots were in the box, and then began the sorting out.

"I will now read the result of the first ballot," announced Captain Putnam, holding up a paper with the figures, and amid a dead silence he began:

Whole number of votes cast 87

Necessary to a choice 44

Fred Garrison has 32

Richard Rover has 8

George Granbury has 15

John Fenwick has 12

"Consequently, nobody is elected. Another vote will be taken immediately after dinner," and then the companies were re-formed and marched into the mess hall.

"Fred Garrison is ahead!" came in a whisper from every side.

"Good for you, Fred!"

"Mumps only got a dozen votes," came from one of the little boys.

"He won't get my vote next time."

"Nor mine," chimed in his chum.

"Don't worry, Dick," whispered Tom. "The final result isn't reached yet. Somebody has got to drop out first."

The dinner finished, the boys gathered in knots to talk the question over. Soon the line was re-formed for a second ballot.

At that moment Fred Garrison stepped forward.

"Fellow students!" he cried. "One word before you vote. I wish to withdraw from the contest, doing so in favor of two of my friends, Dick Rover and George Granbury. I thank those who voted for me before from the bottom of my heart."

"Hurrah for Fred!" came from a score of throats, and a cheer rent the air.

"We won't forget you next time, old man!"

Soon the second ballot was cast, and amid another silence Captain Putnam read it off:

Number of votes cast 87
Necessary to a choice 44
John Fenwick has 7
George Granbury has 23
Richard Rover has 57

"Richard Rover is declared elected second lieutenant of Company A for the balance of this term."

A cheer broke forth, and many of the cadets came up to shake Dick by the hand. Among the number were Fred and George Granbury. "You beat me fairly, Rover," said Granbury, a whole-souled fellow. "I am satisfied—so long—as such a cad as Mumps doesn't get an office."

"Mumps was badly left," put in Tom. "See, he is sneaking off to his room. I rather guess he wishes he hadn't run."

"I thank you all very much," said Dick, his face glowing. "I shall try to do my best as second lieutenant. Three cheers for all of the cadets of Putnam Hall!"

And the cheers broke forth with renewed vigor.

"Dick, you must do the square thing tonight," said Frank some time later.

"What do you mean?" asked the elder Rover.

"When a fellow is elected to an office he is supposed to treat his friends. All of the cadets will be sneaking up to your dormitory some time between ten and twelve o'clock tonight."

"Indeed!" Dick mused for a moment.

"All right—I'll be ready for them, Frank; but mum is the word."

"You will treat?"

"I'll treat every cadet who shows himself and doesn't make any noise."

"Good for you! Then I can spread the word that it is all right?"

"Yes—but, Frank…"

"Well?"

"Beware of Mumps. If he heard of what is going on I think he would try to spoil our game."

"I'll be careful," answered Frank, and hurried off in one direction, while Dick hurried off in another.

Both had scarcely disappeared than Mumps came forth from behind a hall rack which stood close at hand.

"How lucky to overhear their talk," said the sneak. "Will I spoil their game? Well, just wait and see, that's all!"

# CHAPTER XXIV
## PREPARING FOR A MID-NIGHT FEAST

Dick was in a quandary as to how he was to treat all of his friends, and called Sam and Tom to him for consultation.

"I've got a dollar and a quarter," said Sam, "you can use that, and welcome."

"And here is a dollar and ten," added Tom, passing over the amount in ten cent pieces and nickels. "Haven't you any money of your Own?"

"I have two dollars and thirty cents," answered Dick.

"That makes four dollars and sixty-five cents," said Tom, summing up. "That's enough for a pretty fair blow-out."

"So it is, Tom, but where is the stuff to come from? Mrs. Green won't sell it to me."

"That's true."

"And she has her pantries all locked up."

"Oh, pshaw! You don't want to treat the boys on school stuff," said Sam. "Get 'em something from Cedarville—some bottled soda, candies, nuts, and things like that."

"That's the talk, Dick. Let us sneak out after dark and go to Cedarville!" cried Tom. "That would just suit me."

"I'll think it over," answered his big brother slowly.

After supper found most of the cadets indoors, for the night promised to be cold. About half of the boys remained in the library, while the others betook themselves to their rooms.

"Well?" queried Tom, as he approached Dick on the stairs.

"I'm ready, Tom," answered his brother.

"But be careful, or we'll be spotted."

Like a pair of ghosts they glided up the front stairs, along the broad hallway, and down the stairs in the rear. The door was unlocked, and they passed into the yard.

"Let us take Peleg Snuggers into our confidence," whispered Tom. "For a quarter I am certain he'll let us have one of the captain's nags."

"You can test him if you wish," answered Dick, who was doubtful.

Peleg Snuggers was found in the harness room shining up some buckles by the aid of a stable lantern.

"Hullo, Peleg—working rather late," was Tom's greeting.

"Yes, sir—got behind," answered the utility man. "What brought you here?"

"I want a horse, Peleg. Which one can I have?"

"A horse! Did the captain send you?"

Instead of replying Tom held out a silver quarter. "Don't ask questions, Peleg, but just let me take a horse for an hour or two, that's a good man."

"Can't do it, Master Rover—against orders, sir."

"Oh, yes, you can. We won't hurt the beast. We are bound to get to Cedarville and back before ten o'clock. Do you want us to drop on the road from exhaustion and be frozen to death?" and Tom put the question in all seriousness.

"No, no, certainly not!"

"Then bring out a horse. That black will do. Here, take the quarter, Peleg, and much obliged to you. Hurry up."

"Was there ever such a boy!" grumbled the man; but, nevertheless, he arose and got the black horse ready for them, hooking the animal to a small cutter.

"Remember, if the captain learns of this, I don't know nothing about it...," he called out, as the two boys drove off by a back way, out of sight of the main building of the institution.

"Peleg is all right, if you know how to handle him," said Tom, as he took the reins from Dick.

"I'll let him out a bit, and we'll drive to Cedarville in a jiffy."

"Tom, you're getting more cheeky every day," was Dick's comment, yet he was far from displeased over what his brother had accomplished.

Away went the cutter, the roads being now in an excellent condition. Soon Putnam Hall was left far behind, and they came within sight of the Stanhope homestead.

"I'd like to stop for just a minute," said Dick, but Tom shook his head.

"We want to get to Cedarville before the shops close," said the younger brother.

"We can stop on the way back—if we have time," and they continued on their way.

Both knew Cedarville "like a book," as Tom expressed it, having been there so many times before. They drove straight to the largest confectionery in the village.

"A pound of chocolates, a pound of marshmallows, a pound of iced fruits, and five pounds of best mixed candies," said Dick, and the articles were quickly put up for him.

"How much?"

"A dollar and thirty cents, please."

The bill was paid, and they hurried to another store, where they purchased two dozen bottles of soda water, a dozen bottles of root beer, and five pounds of mixed nuts. Tom wanted to buy some cigarettes for such of the cadets as might wish to smoke, but Dick shook his head at this.

"No, that's going too far," he said. "We'll have a respectable spread, and that's enough."

Inside of half an hour they had started on the return, the various articles purchased stowed safely away in the back of the cutter.

"We'll have at least fifteen minutes to spare," said Dick, and waited as patiently as possible until the Stanhope homestead again appeared. As soon as they gained the entrance to the garden, Dick hopped out, ran up the path to the porch, and rang the bell. Dora Stanhope answered his summons.

"Oh, Dick, is that you?" she cried. "Come in."

"I can't stay but a few minutes, Dora," he answered as he entered the hall. "I must get back to the academy. I thought I would just stop to see how you are getting on."

"Oh, everything is the same, Dick."

"I heard the marriage was to take place this week."

"Yes."

"Let me tell you something," went on the boy, and told her of the letter to be sent from Chicago to Josiah Crabtree.

"Oh, I hope he gets it and goes!" exclaimed Dora quickly, and her face brightened a bit.

"Send me word if he does," said Dick.

He remained for ten minutes longer, but what was said and done need not be mentioned here. When he left his heart was all aglow, while Dora was blushing deeply. "Best girl in the world," he murmured. "What an awfully nice young fellow," was Dora's thought.

"Hurry up!" cried Tom from the sleigh, when his big brother put in an appearance again. "I'm most frozen stiff!" And on went the cutter, the horse feeling quite fresh after his rest.

"I'll go ahead and see if the coast is clear," said Dick, when they reached the vicinity of the stable, and he leaped into the snow. It did not take long to walk to the barn. He was gone but a few minutes, and came back on a run.

"We are in for it!" he cried. "Mr. Strong is down at the stable talking to Peleg Snuggers."

"Great Caesar! What's to do?"

"Get the stuff out of the sleigh first and hide it near the Hall in the snow," answered Dick. "Be quick!"

His advice was followed, Tom carrying the soda water and root beer and Dick the other things. All were hidden in a snow bank—directly under the dormitory window.

This accomplished, Dick led the horse up to the back of the stable and unhitched him. He could hear George Strong and the utility man talking less than twenty feet away.

"Very well, Snuggers, I'll be back shortly," he heard, coming from the head assistant, and Strong walked from the stable toward the Hall.

In a twinkle Dick ran around the stable corner. "Quick, Peleg, here is the horse, all unhooked. Put him in his stall. The cutter is back there, out of sight," and as the hired man took possession of the animal, the youth ran off, to join his brother at the entrance to Putnam Hall.

"The door is locked!" groaned Tom.

"Something is wrong."

Without replying, Dick ran around to a spot under the dormitory window. Making a soft snowball, he threw it against the glass, and followed this by several others. Presently the window was thrown up, and Sam, Fred, and Larry showed their heads.

"Say, you fellows, help us up!" cried Dick softly. "There is a wash line in the closet—the one my Aunt Martha insisted on tying around my trunk when we came here last summer."

There was a scramble in the room, and presently the end of the line was thrown out. It was new and strong, and quite capable of supporting either of the lads' weight.

"You go first, Tom but be quick!" said Dick softly, and his brother caught hold and went up with ease, bracing one foot after another against the rough stonework and projecting bricks. Then the rope came down a second time and Dick ascended.

Hardly were the boys in the room than there came a loud knocking on the door.

"It's Mr. Strong!" gasped Sam. "What shall we do now? It looks as if we were a caught!"

# CHAPTER XXV
## MUMPS IS TAUGHT A LESSON

The cadets stared blankly at each other. Only two of them were undressed; the others had all of their clothing on.

It was time for the head assistant to go the rounds, to see that all was right for the night. Should he be allowed to enter the dormitory he would certainly "smell a mouse," and perhaps knock all of their plans for a feast in the head.

"Off with your clothing, all of you!" whispered Tom. "I'll manage this affair. Pretend to be asleep."

"But, Tom, it's my fault—" began Dick, when his younger brother cut him short.

"Into the bed—I'll be all right, Dick."

Satisfied that Tom had some plan in his head for smoothing matters over, the other boys disrobed with marvelous rapidity and crept into their beds. While this was going on the knocking an the door continued.

"Boys, open the door!" said George Strong. "Open the door, do you hear?"

"Answer him!" whispered Tom to Larry, whose bed was nearest him. "Pretend you have just awoke," and he flung himself on the floor, with one of a pair of big rubber boots in each hand.

"Oh—er—Mr. Strong, is that you?"

"Yes, open the door."

"Why—er—is it locked?

"Yes."

At once Larry tumbled from his bed, unlocked the door and stood there rubbing his eyes. "Excuse me, Sir, for not hearing you before."

"I want to know what the meaning is of the noise in here?" said George Strong severely, as he gazed around the dimly lit apartment, for the lamp was turned low. "You boys are—gracious me! What's this?"

The teacher started back in genuine surprise, and his words aroused all of the boys in the beds, who followed his gaze in equal wonder.

For in the center of the floor sat Tom, his eyes tightly closed, a rubber boot in each hand, and rocking backward and forward with great rapidity, as if rowing.

"Two lengths ahead!" muttered Tom. "I'll beat you yet, Larry! Three lengths! Oh, but this is a dandy race! Pull away, you can't beat me! Oh! There goes an oar," and, bang! went one of the rubber boots against the base board, and Tom made a leap as if diving into the water after it, sprawling and spluttering as he pretended to swim.

"He's got the nightmare again!" shouted out Sam, quick to understand Tom's dodge. "Tom, wake up there!"

"The nightmare!" echoed Mr. Strong. "Is it possible? Poor boy! Wake up, Thomas!" and he caught Tom by the shoulder and shook him and finally set him on his feet.

"The oar—I will have the— Oh!" Tom opened his eyes and stared around him blankly. "Why—er—what's up?"

"My boy, you've had the nightmare," answered the teacher kindly.

"Nightmare!"

"I told you not to eat that pie tonight," put in Sam. "He saved his pie from dinner, and ate it just before we came up here,"—which was true.

"Er—I thought I was on the lake racing Larry Colby," murmured Tom and hid his face as if in embarrassment. "What did I do?" he faltered.

"You almost raised the roof, that's what you did," answered Dick. "You had better send home for some of those digestion tablets you used to take," and then he hid his face in the blankets to keep from laughing out loud.

"I will." Tom turned to George Strong. "Excuse me, Mr. Strong, I am sorry I have caused you so much trouble."

"How do you feel now?" questioned the assistant anxiously.

"Oh, I'm all right now."

"Well, then, go to bed; and I trust you sleep more soundly for the balance of the night," said the teacher; and he remained in the room until Tom was tucked in, when he went off, taking the key of the door with him.

"Tom, you're a brick!" came from Frank, when the teacher was out of hearing. "What a head you have on your shoulders!"

"Strong took the key of the door," said Fred.

"I don't like that."

"Shove a chair-back up under the knob," suggested Dick, and this was done, the chair thus making an excellent brace.

"Now to get that stuff in," said Dick, donning his clothing with all possible speed. "I shouldn't wonder if the soda and root beer are frozen as hard as a rock."

He was soon ready to descend, and the others lowered him by aid of the wash line. Then the boxes and packages were hoisted up, and Dick came after.

A few minutes later came a slight tapping on the door, repeated three times. It was a signal, and Sam opened the door, admitting George Granbury and seven other cadets from dormitory No. 2. The occupants of several other dormitories followed.

"Are we to have Mumps and his crowd in here?" asked one of the newcomers.

"I don't want Mumps," answered Dick. "Not because he ran against me, but because he was Baxter's toady and is a regular sneak."

"Little Luke Walton and Mark Gross voted for you, Dick," said Harry Blossom. "They ought to be invited."

"All right, tell them to come in, and anybody else who wishes, outside of Mumps," answered Dick.

The young captain went off, and soon returned with six boys of Sam's age or younger.

"Mumps is awfully mad," he announced. "My idea is, he is going to cause us trouble if he can."

"We'll wax him good if he does!" cried Tom. "Say, Sam, let us watch him," and he hurried into the hallway, while the others attacked the several good things Dick had provided for them.

Tom and Sam had been in the dark hallway but two minutes when the door of Mumps' dormitory opened and the sneak came out, wearing his slippers and his long overcoat. He glided swiftly toward the side stairs leading to Captain Putnam's private apartments.

"He's going to peach!" whispered Tom, "Come on, Sam, let us capture the enemy!" and he hurried after Mumps and caught him by the arm.

"Hi! who is this?" demanded the sneak, turning in fear. Then, as Tom and Sam confronted him, his face grew white.

"Come with us, Mumps, we want to treat you," answered Tom readily, into whose head another trick had entered.

"I don't want any of your treat," growled the sneak. "Let me go."

"Oh, you must come," urged Tom. "We have a fine bottle of root beer and a lot of candied fruit for you."

If there was one thing that Mumps liked, it was root beer, while he knew candied fruit was very rich eating. Accordingly he hesitated.

"I'll get all I can first and tell on them afterward," he thought, and allowed Tom, and Sam to conduct him into the dormitory occupied by the Metropolitan Sextet.

"Here is Mumps come to join us!" cried Tom, as he introduced the sneak into the room and he winked at Dick. "Now, Mumps, sit down and make yourself at home, and I'll get something for you," and he motioned the sneak to a position at the head of his bed.

He hurried off, and presently came back to Mumps with a fine slice of candied orange. The sneak was greedy, and instantly transferred the entire slice to his mouth and began to chew it vigorously.

"Oh!" he cried presently, and drew down his face in disgust.

"What's the matter, Mumps?" asked Sam.

"This orange tastes like kerosene!" spluttered Mumps, and rushed to the window. As he put out his head, Tom pointed to the sneak and then to the lamp at which he had "flavored" the candied fruit. "We'll get square just wait," he whispered. "You gave me that piece on purpose," howled the sneak, as soon as he had cleared his mouth. "Oh, what an awful dose! Somebody give me a drink of water."

"The water is all gone, Mumps," answered Tom. "Awfully sorry. Have a glass of root beer," and he poured out a tumbler full.

Willing to drink anything to take that taste out of his mouth, the sneak took the tumbler and gulped down about half of the root beer.

The remainder was about to follow, when suddenly he stopped short. "Oh, my!"

"Awfully good, isn't it?" put in Dick.

"Good? It tastes like salt water!" snorted Mumps. And he was not far wrong, for Tom had taken the pains to put a lot of salt in to the glass before filling it up.

"Why, that is the best root beer I ever tasted," put in Larry. "It's as sweet as sugar. Let me taste your glass, Mumps."

"Do so with pleasure," and the sneak passed it over. Larry pretended to take a gulp. "Fine! Couldn't be better. Isn't that so, Frank?" and he passed the glass to Harrington. "It's certainly as good as mine, and that's O. K.," answered Frank; and then George Granbury took the tumbler and declared the root beer was even better than what he had had previously.

"It's certainly your stomach, Mumps, my boy," said Tom. "You look kind of funny—just like a fellow I knew who got the smallpox."

"He does look like a fellow getting the smallpox," put in Dick. "Mumps, does your tongue feel dry-like?"

"Dry, of course it is dry—and salty," growled Mumps, but he began to grow uneasy.

"Let me see your tongue," put in Sam, who happened to have a blue pencil in his pocket. As he spoke he broke off some of the blue point and crumbled it in his fingers.

"My tongue is all right," answered Mumps. Nevertheless, he held it out; and Sam slyly dropped the bluing on it.

"It's as blue as indigo!" he exclaimed, "Look into the glass for yourself."

Somewhat against his will, Mumps strode over to the looking glass. As he noted the condition of his tongue, he grew very pale and began to tremble.

"It is blue," he whined, "and—and—I feel sick all over. Oh, say, do you think I really am getting the smallpox?"

For an instant there was a dead silence. Then the boys could hold in no longer, and a long but smothered laugh showed the sneak how completely he had been sold.

# CHAPTER XXVI
## A LIVELY GAME OF BASEBALL

If ever a boy was mad clear through that boy was the sneak of Putnam Hall. As the laugh ended, Mumps shook his fist at one and another of his tormentors.

"Think you are smart, don't you?" he spluttered in his rage. "I'll fix you all! I'll go and tell Captain Putnam all about this spread, and then maybe you won't catch it!"

"Mumps, keep quiet," said Dick, placing himself between the enraged one and the door. "Make too much noise, and I'll promise you the worst drubbing you ever received."

"If you peach on me, I'll give you a second whipping," added Tom.

"This is a gentlemanly affair," put in Larry.

"The boy who gives us away gets a thrashing from me."

"Ditto myself," said Frank; and several others said the same. All looked so determined that Mumps fell back in alarm.

"You let me go," he whined. "I don't want to stay here any longer."

"You can't go until you promise to keep quiet," said Dick.

"And you'll promise right now," cried Tom, seizing a pitcher of ice water that had been hidden under one of the stands. Leaping on a bed he held the pitcher over Mumps' head.

"Promise, quick, or I'll let her go!" he went on.

"Oh, don't!" yelled Mumps, as a few drops of the water landed on his head and ran down his neck.

"Do you promise to keep silent?" demanded Dick.

"Yes, yes!"

"All right. Now mind, if you break that promise you are in for at least ten good whippings."

"Somebody else may give you away," said Mumps craftily.

"No one will. If Captain Putnam hears about this it will be only through you. So beware, Mumps, if you value your hide!" And then the sneak was allowed to go. Five minutes later the spread came to an end, the muss was cleared away, and every cadet sought his couch, to rest if not to sleep.

It is possible that Captain Putnam and George Strong suspected something, yet as the cadets seemed none the worse for the festivities the next day, nothing was said on the subject. "Boys will be boys," smiled the captain to his head assistant; and there the whole matter dropped.

Several days later, while some of the cadets were down at the cove clearing off a portion of the ice for skating, Mrs. Stanhope's man-of-all-work came over with a note for Dick from Dora. The Rover boys all read the note with deep interest.

"I have good news [so ran the communication]. Mr. Crabtree has gone to Chicago, and the marriage has been postponed until next summer. You do not know how glad I am. Of course there will be trouble when Mr. Crabtree learns how he has been fooled, but mother has promised me to remain single until August or September, and I know she will keep that promise. I thank all of you very much for what you have done. Yesterday I saw Dan Baxter, who seems to be hanging around this neighborhood a good deal. He wanted to speak to me, but I did not give him the chance. I wish he would go away, for he looks to me like a very evil-minded person. It is strange, but Mr. Crabtree thinks a good deal of him, and has told my mother so. He says it is nonsense to put Mr. Baxter down as a criminal."

"Baxter stopping around here…" mused Dick. "What can he be up to?"

"He had better clear out," said Sam. The matter was discussed for some time, but nothing came of it.

Skating lasted for nearly a month, and then both the ice and the snow melted away as if by magic. Soon spring was at hand, and the early flowers began to show themselves in Mrs. Green's little garden, which was the housekeeper's one pride.

Dick had seen Dora once in that time. The girl had told him about how Josiah Crabtree had searched in vain for the college mentioned in the bogus letter.

"He said I played the trick," were Dora's words. "He wants mother to send me to some strict boarding school."

"And are you going?" had been Dick's question.

"No, I shall remain with mother. After she is married again I do not know what will become of me," and as Dora's eyes filled with tears Dick caught her hand.

"Don't worry, Dora," had been his words. "I will help you, and it is bound to come up right in the end."

As soon as summer was at hand, the Putnam Hall baseball club received a challenge from the Pornell club to play them a game at either school grounds.

"They want to square accounts for the football defeat," said Fred. "Well, the only thing to do is to accept the challenge," and the acceptance was sent without delay, the game to be played on the Putnam Hall grounds, Captain Putnam having promised the cadets his aid in building a grandstand. The lumber came out of a boathouse that had been torn down to make place for a new structure, and as many of the cadets took to carpentering naturally, the grandstand was quite a creditable affair.

Frank Harrington was captain and catcher for the Putnam Hall team. Tom was pitcher, while Larry played first base, Dick second, and Sam was down in center, to use those nimble legs of his should occasion require. Fred was shortstop, and the balance of the club was made up of the best players the school afforded.

The Saturday chosen for the game was an ideal one, clear and not too warm. The students from Pornell arrived early, and so did the other visitors, and by two o'clock the grounds were crowded.

As before a parade was had. Then the umpire came out and gave each team fifteen minutes for practice.

"We're in luck," said Dick, when Putnam Hall won the toss and took last innings. In a moment more they were in the field, and the Ump called out: "Play!"

As was natural, Pornell had put its heaviest batters at the head of their list, and it is possible Tom was a bit nervous as he twirled the ball and sent it in toward the home plate.

"Ball one!" came the decision, and again the sphere came in.
"Ball two!" said the umpire.

"Take it easy, Tom!" called out Dick. "Lots of time, remember."

The next was a strike. Then came a foul, and then a hard drive to left field, and amid a wild, cheering the Pornell batsman gained second base in safety.

"That's the way to do it, Cornwall! Keep it up, Snader!"

The second player now came up, and again the ball came in. Tom was as nervous as before, and another hit was made, and the player covered first, while the man on second went to third.

"Tom, do be careful," whispered Frank, walking down to him. "Don't let that fellow in," and he nodded in the direction of the first runner.

The third player was now at the bat. Two balls and two strikes were counted against him and then came a foul, high up in the air, which Frank caught with ease.

"One out, and two on base! That's not so bad."

Again the ball came in. "One strike!" said the umpire. "I want a high ball!" growled the batter. Again the ball was delivered. "Two strikes!" Then the ball came in again. "Three strikes! Batter out!" And Tom got a rousing cheer for striking out the Pornellite.

But the two men were still on first and third, with one more man to put out.

"Take care!" whispered Larry, and the basemen all moved up closer. One strike, and then came a high fly, far out in center field.

"Run, Sam! Don't miss that!" came in a yell. "Run! run!"

And Sam did run, knowing that if he missed the ball the Pornell team would score two runs, if not three. It was going far down the field, but he was after it, and just as it came down, he made a leap and—clutched the sphere with his left hand.

"He has it! Hurrah! No runs this innings for Pornell!" And the Putnamites howled themselves hoarse, while their opponents had nothing to say.

But the players from the rival academy had a fine battery, and it was impossible to "get onto" their pitcher's curves during that first innings. The players went out in one, two, three order, leaving the score 0 to 0.

"It's going to be a close game," said an old player from, Cedarville. "I'm not betting on either side."

The second innings passed without any scoring being done. In the third innings the Pornell team made two runs. In the next innings Putnam Hall pulled a single run "out of the fire," as Dick put it, for it was his tally, made on a slide halfway from third base.

After this there were more "goose eggs," until the end of the eighth inning when the score became a tie, 2 to 2.

One more inning for each side, and the excitement became intense.

"We must prevent them from scoring, by all means," said Frank as they took the field, while the first batter of the Pornellites came to the plate; and amid a breathless silence the final innings began.

# CHAPTER XXVII
## OFF FOR THE SUMMER ENCAMPMEMT

The present situation was enough to make any pitcher nervous, and it must be confessed that Tom could scarcely control himself. "A wild pitch, and it's all up with our side," he thought, as he took his place in the "box."

"One ball!" That was the verdict as the sphere landed in Frank's hands. "Two balls!" came immediately after.

Frank paused, then rolled the ball to Tom. "Do be careful," whispered Dick. "Take your time."

"Perhaps we had better put Larry in the box," suggested another player, but Tom shook his head determinedly. "I'll stick it out!"

"One strike!" The batter had tried, but failed to hit the sphere. Tom felt more hopeful, but immediately after came three balls and then four balls, and amid a cheer from his friends the Pornell player walked to first base.

The second man at the bat went out on a foul, and the cadets cheered this time. Then came a strong hit to left field, and in came one run.

"Hurrah! 3 to 2 in Pornell's favor!"

"You've got 'em on the run now, boys; keep it up!"

Two balls, and the next batter knocked a hot liner to Fred. It came along like lightning, but Fred wore a "do-or-die" look and made a dive for it—and held on, although his hands stung as if scorched with fire.

"Hurrah! Two out! Now for the third, and then knock out that lead of one run!"

Alas! This was easier said than done. The next player gained first, and so did the youth to follow. Then came a heavy hit, and the score went up to 5 to 2. But that was the last of it, so far as Pornell was concerned.

"Now, Putnam Hall, see what you can do!"

Larry was at the bat, and cautious about striking. "One strike!" called the umpire, as the boy let a good ball go by. Another real strike followed, and then Larry caught the sphere fairly and squarely, drove it far into left field, and made a home run.

"A homer! Wasn't that great!"

"That makes the score 5 to 3. Keep it up, Putnam Hall!"

The home run was very encouraging, and now Dick came forward with his ashen stick. He had one strike called on him and then managed to make a clean one-base hit.

Another player, named Forwell, took stand next. The pitcher for the Pornell team was now as nervous as Tom bad been and suddenly Forwell was hit in the arm by the ball.

"Dead ball!" cried the umpire. "Take your base," and Forwell went to first, while Larry marched to second.

Then Sam came to the bat, but his first strike was a foul, caught by the third baseman. Another out followed, made by the captain, much to his chagrin. The score now stood 5 to 3, with two players on base and two out. One more out and the match would come to an end, unless the score was a tie.

"Tom Rover to the bat!" called the score-keeper, and Tom marched to the plate. A strike and two balls, and he made as clean a one-base hit as had his elder brother.

"Three on base and two out!" came the cry.

"Now, Pornell, be careful!"

Fred Garrison was the next of the team to come forward. All eyes were centered upon Fred. "Be careful, oh, be careful!" pleaded Frank. "Don't get out as I did!"

"One strike!" cried the umpire as the ball whizzed over the plate. "Ball one!" came a moment later. "Strike two!" was immediately added.

Bang! the ball had come on again, and Fred had hit it with all of the force at his command. It shot past second base and toward centerfield. "Run! run!" yelled Frank, and the crowd joined in, as Dick started for home, followed by Forwell and Tom. The center fielder fumbled the ball, and the four runners came in one right on top of the other.

"Putnam Hall has won!"

"Say, but wasn't that a great game?"

"Hurrah! hurrah! hurrah!" came from the cadets and their friends.

It was a great time for the boys. They gave three cheers for their opponents, but the Pornellites felt their second defeat too keenly, and as quickly as they could they left the grounds, and quarter of an hour later were on their way home.

After this contest matters moved along quietly until June. In the meantime the cadets studied up with all diligence for the examinations soon to take place. All of our friends passed creditably, Dick standing second in his class, Tom fourth and Sam third in their classes. Captain Putnam and George Strong heartily approved of the showing made.

"That Tom Rover is full of fun," was the captain's comment, "but he knows how to study as well as how to play jokes."

Mumps was almost at the foot of his class. The sneak had hardly any friends left, and he announced that he was going to leave Putnam Hall never to return—for which no one was particularly sorry.

Immediately after the examinations it was announced that the entire school would march to a place called Brierroot Grove, where they would go into their annual encampment for two weeks. At once all of the cadets were in a bustle, and soon uniforms were brushed up, buckles and buttons polished, knapsacks packed, and rifles oiled and cleaned.

"Makes a fellow feel as if he was going off to the war!" observed Sam. "I don't know but what I would like to be a soldier some day."

The battalion marched away one Monday morning, with flags flying, drums beating loudly, and the fifers blowing away upon "Yankee Doodle" with all of their might. The route was the lake road, and many of the farmhouses passed were decorated in honor of the departure. As they passed the Stanhope homestead, Dora and Mrs. Stanhope came forth and waved their handkerchiefs, and Dick, as second lieutenant of Company A, could not resist the temptation to wave his sword at them.

The camping-out spot was reached that afternoon at five o'clock. The provision wagon and that loaded with the tents had already come up, and soon the cadets were putting up their tents, while the cooking detail was preparing supper. The evening meal consisted of nothing but bread, coffee, and beef stew, but never did plain fare taste better, with such pure mountain air for sauce.

"It's just boss!" said Tom on the second day in camp. "Living in a tent suits me to death."

The next day, however, he changed his tune, for it rained in torrents, and everybody got soaked to the skin.

"Ugh!" said Tom. "I wasn't thinking of this when I said it suited me to death." All made the best of it, and luckily the storm did not last over twenty-four hours, when the sun came out warmly, and that was the last of the rain while the encampment lasted.

A week had passed by when one afternoon Dick, Tom, and Sam received permission to visit the town of Rootville, a mile away. They were not to be gone not over three hours, and were to purchase some medicine needed by several cadets who had taken cold during the damp spell.

The boys walked to Rootville in high spirits, and readily procured the drugs desired, then they wandered around from place to place, taking in the sights.

There was a depot, and as natural they drifted thither, and into the waiting room. Here almost the first persons they saw was Arnold Baxter and Buddy the tramp thief.

"Gracious!" burst from Dick's lips, and then he pulled Tom and Sam back. "Here is a chance at last to arrest that thief!"

"That's so!" cried Tom. "Wait, I saw a policeman outside. I'll call him," and he darted off. While Dick and Sam awaited Tom's reappearance, they noticed that Baxter and Buddy were holding a conversation of great interest.

"I will pay you well if you will help me in this deal," Arnold Baxter was saying.

"I'll do all I can," answered Buddy Girk. "But what of your son Dan?"

"Dan is not to be depended upon," answered Arnold Baxter. "He robbed me of two hundred dollars and skipped out for Chicago."

"Humph!" murmured Dick. "Here is certainly news of Dan Baxter that is very much to his discredit. I hope I and Dora and the rest never hear of him again."

Some other folks now came into the depot, and Arnold Baxter and Buddy lowered their voices, so that Dick and Sam could hear nothing further.

Soon Tom arrived, followed by the policeman, who looked anxiously at the two men.

"You say they are thieves?" he asked of Dick.

"The short man is. He stole my watch."

"What of the other?"

"He is a bad man too—although it may be hard to prove it."

At once the crowd approached the evil pair, and the officer caught Buddy Girk by the arm, "I want you," he said in a low, firm voice.

The thief turned swiftly, and as he saw himself confronted by Dick and the officer of the law his face fell.

"I ain't done nothing'!" he cried, and tried to break away, but the officer at once overpowered him and brought forth a pair of handcuffs.

"You'll put these on," he said grimly, and spite his protestations Buddy Girk was handcuffed.

"Hold on!" cried Dick, as Arnold Baxter started to run. He made a clutch for the man, but Baxter was too quick for him and slipped through the crowd and out of the depot. Instantly Dick made after him.

# CHAPTER XXVIII
## THE RECOVERY OF THE WATCH—CONCLUSION

Arnold Baxter hesitated but a moment on gaining the depot platform. A freight train was passing the station at a slow rate of speed, and, running to an empty car which stood wide open, he leaped on board.

Dick was close behind him, and as the man boarded the freight car caught him by the leg. As Dick held on like a bulldog there was nothing left for Arnold Baxter to do but to drag the youth up behind him.

"You imp!" he snarled, as the two faced each other on the car floor. "What do you mean by following me in this fashion?"

"And what do you mean by running away in this fashion?" panted Dick.

"I have a right to do as I please."

"And so have!"

"You have no right to follow me."

"That remains to be seen, Arnold Baxter. I would like to ask you a few questions."

"Would you, indeed?" sneered the tall man.

"Yes. I won't waste words. Were you and my father enemies years ago?"

At this direct question Arnold Baxter scowled darkly. "Yes, if you are anxious to know," he muttered.

"I fancied as much. You tried to swindle him out of some Western mining property."

"The boot was on the other leg—he tried to swindle me—ran off to Africa with my papers, I think, or else left them somewhere where I can't find them."

"I do not believe you, for my father was an honest man, while you are the boon companion of a thief."

"Have a care, boy—I won't stand everything!" snarled Arnold Baxter, his eyes gleaning like those of an angry cat.

"I am not afraid of you, Arnold Baxter. I shall hand you over to the police at our next stopping place!"

"Will you!" hissed the man, and leaped at Dick, bearing him down to the car floor. At once his hand sought the lad's throat.

"I've a good mind to choke the life out of you," he went on. "I hate you all—everyone who bears the name of Rover!"

"Le—let up!" gasped Dick, growing purple in the face, while his eyes bulged from their sockets.

"I'll pitch you off!" was Arnold Baxter's answer, and suddenly he lifted Dick up in his strong arms and stepped to the open doorway. They were passing over a trestle spanning a wide gully, at the bottom of which were bushes, rocks, and a tiny mountain stream.

"Don't!" cried Dick, and snatched at the handle of the car door. He had just clutched it, when Arnold Baxter launched forth his body into space.

The next instant, and while Baxter stood by the edge of the door, the long train swung around a sharp curve. There was a quick jerk, and with a yell of fright which sounded in Dick's ears for days afterward, Arnold Baxter slipped through the doorway and went tumbling head foremost down into the gully!

Dick shut his eyes at the sight and clung fast mechanically. Then, as soon as he could recover, he swung himself into the car. He could not stand, and sank like a lump of lead to the car floor unconscious.

When he recovered, several train hands surrounded him, and his face was wet from the water they had poured over him. It was fully an hour before he could tell his story, and then a hand-car was sent back to the spot where Arnold Baxter had had his terrible fall.

The rascal was found at the foot of the gully, a leg and several ribs broken and otherwise bruised. He was carried to the hand-car like one dead, and later on transferred to a hospital at Ithaca. Here it was announced that he might possibly recover, although this was exceedingly doubtful.

"He's a bad one," said Tom, when he heard Dick's story. "I would like to know what Buddy Girk has to say about him."

Buddy had been taken to the Rootville jail and searched, and a pawn-ticket for the stolen watch found in his vest pocket. The ticket was on a Middletown pawnbroker, and showed that fifteen dollars had been loaned on the timepiece. Buddy had more than this amount in his pocket, and some time later the money was forwarded to the pawnbroker, and then the precious watch and chain came back to Dick, in as good a condition as ever.

"I haven't got nuthin' to say," said Buddy, when Dick tried to make him talk. "I didn't steal the watch, and I didn't do nothin'."

"You won't tell me anything about Arnold Baxter?" questioned Dick.

"Ain't got nuthin' to say," repeated Buddy, who was planning to escape from jail that very night.

And escape he did, through a window the bars of which were bent and broken. The authorities searched for him for nearly a week, but the search proved unavailing.

"I don't care particularly," said Dick, in commenting on the affair. "I have my watch back and that's the main thing."

"But Buddy ought to be punished. Now if it was Arnold Baxter who had gotten away—after that terrible fall—I wouldn't say a word," answered Tom.

The encampment came to an end in a blaze of glory on the Forth of July, with firecrackers and fireworks galore. The cadets "cut up like wild Indians" until after midnight, and Captain Putnam gave them a free rein. "Independence Day comes but once a year," he said. "And I would not give much for the boy who is not patriotic."

"You are right there, captain," returned George Strong. "Our boys are true blue, every one of them."

Out on the parade ground the cadets were singing loudly and marching at the same time. Everyone was in the best of high spirits, and it was a time never to be forgotten.

Here I must bring to a close, for the present, the story of the Rover Boys' doings at Putnam Hall and elsewhere. We have seen how Dick was robbed of his watch and how he recovered the timepiece; how the boys joined the other cadets, and what friends and enemies they made; and we have likewise entered into many a sport and contest with them.

With the termination of the encampment the school term came to an end, and the Rover boys returned to their home with their uncle and aunt. But more adventures were in store for them, and these will be related in another volume, to be entitled "The Rover Boys on the Ocean; or, a Chase for Fortune." In this volume we will meet all of our old friends, and also learn more concerning Josiah Crabtree and his little plot to marry Mrs. Stanhope and obtain the money the lady was holding in trust for Dora. We shall likewise meet Dan Baxter and his toady Mumps, and learn much concerning a thrilling chase on the ocean and its happy results.

But for the present all went well. The boys arrived at the homestead two days after the Fourth and were met at the door by their Uncle Randolph and Aunt Martha.

"Welcome home, all of you!" cried Randolph Rover. And as their aunt kissed them, he continued, "And what do you think of your school?"

"What do we think?" repeated Tom.

"Why, we think Putnam Hall is the best boys school on earth!"

And Dick and Sam agreed with him.

**The End**